Hoosier Writers
2011

Hoosier Writers 2011

A Collection of Poetry and Fiction

Lowell R. Torres

iUniverse, Inc.
Bloomington

Hoosier Writers 2011
A Collection of Poetry and Fiction

Copyright © 2011 by Lowell R. Torres.

All rights reserved. No part of this book may be used or reproduced by any means, graphic, electronic, or mechanical, including photocopying, recording, taping or by any information storage retrieval system without the written permission of the publisher except in the case of brief quotations embodied in critical articles and reviews.

iUniverse books may be ordered through booksellers or by contacting:

iUniverse
1663 Liberty Drive
Bloomington, IN 47403
www.iuniverse.com
1-800-Authors (1-800-288-4677)

Because of the dynamic nature of the Internet, any web addresses or links contained in this book may have changed since publication and may no longer be valid. The views expressed in this work are solely those of the author and do not necessarily reflect the views of the publisher, and the publisher hereby disclaims any responsibility for them.

Any people depicted in stock imagery provided by Thinkstock are models, and such images are being used for illustrative purposes only.
Certain stock imagery © Thinkstock.

ISBN: 978-1-4620-3754-4 (sc)
ISBN: 978-1-4620-3946-3 (ebk)

Printed in the United States of America

iUniverse rev. date: 07/22/2011

Contents

Foreword

I fell in love with writing and the world of literature when I was thirteen. I lived in the Dorie Miller Housing Projects of Gary, Indiana and attended Dunbar-Pulaski Middle School. A tall and skinny buck-toothed white kid with a Spanish last name, I didn't exactly fit in with the rest of the approximately 700 other students (only six of whom were Caucasian or Latino).

Life was far from pleasant, but I'm not writing to complain about how tough I had it. Of the five children in my family I probably had it the easiest. I was a nerd, but I was also six feet tall and over time perfected such a menacing scowl that only the biggest, meanest and dumbest of my peers thought to escalate their harassment beyond the verbal level. While I faced an endless onslaught of insults and a barrage of various projectiles ranging from spitballs to erasers, there were only three truly physical confrontations.

My siblings weren't so lucky. My older brother dropped out of high school after he was attacked in a hallway, his new pair of Air Jordan's ripped off of his feet. My younger sisters and brother faced monthly if not weekly and—at times—daily beatings by various groups of children.

To say I hated living there would be an understatement. School was daily harassment. Home was a toxic stew of misery; the pain, humiliation and anger of seven people packed into a nine-hundred square-foot cockroach-infested apartment. If you stepped out our front door and walked across the street you'd be standing about twenty feet away from a group of gangbanging crack dealers who "represented" Dorie Miller. Their presence was a constant source of intimidation and fear.

I only dredge up these memories, nearly twenty years old now, to say they were all worth it for this:

"Over the weekend I want you to write a poem."

I groaned along with most of the rest of the class.

Eighth grade Advanced English was with Mrs. Williams, a kindly older woman who still took obvious joy in her job despite the daily contempt she faced from some of her students. And I certainly felt contempt at that time. A poem? Um, no thanks.

My Gramps had recently bought my brother the new *Mortal Kombat* game for Super Nintendo. My weekend plans involved trying to reach the villainous Shang Tsung and his monstrous henchman Goro. Writing a stupid girly poem had no place in those plans.

So of course I waited until Sunday night to even start thinking about the assignment. I sat there for a good half an hour just staring at the paper with no clue how to begin. I was feeling rather sorry for myself, as I usually did during that time. My range of moods didn't often vary beyond anger and angst. The angst was strong on that day, so I started with the line,

Now and then I begin to say
Why in the world was I born this way

And something happened. A spark that in time would ignite a fire. The poem that followed was poorly worded to fit the rhyme scheme, and didn't always make sense, but it brought about a feeling I couldn't explain. I had taken some of the tortured thoughts that lay within me and dragged them out onto the page, and as a result some of those demons felt partially exorcised.

It was not a very good poem, but as I would find out the next day, the words had a certain power to them. Mrs. Williams volunteered me to stand up and read the poem to the class, something I was not fond of, and the snickers of my classmates made the idea even less appealing. So far most of the poems read were variations of the "Roses are red" diddy. My favorite up til that point went something like, "Roses are red like Michael Jordan's jersey. I wish he was my dad. That would be rad."

I stood up in front of the class, already blushing, and read my poem. The snickers stopped, and an amazing thing took its place:

sobbing. Two girls, one of whom I was madly in infatuation with, were crying quite openly and even stood up to applaud. Mrs. Williams had a look of sadness mingled with pride and asked for my permission to try to get the poem published.

I was flabbergasted, and for the first time realized the line I'd heard from teachers several times before was true. Words do have power, and that was a great thing to someone who felt powerless most of the time. My relationship with the written word had begun, and has been an up and down relationship since.

Early on I wrote terribly campy short stories that were almost direct rip-offs of movies or books I liked, but I would become the protagonist or occasionally antagonist. Horror was my preferred genre. Alien abductions and serial killers. Werewolves and vampires and zombies, oh my! Occasionally I would go back to poetry and write the kind of "emo" poems you might find in any teenager's notebook, but fiction was where it was at.

My first real effort at writing came my sophomore year of high school. My family had been through some turbulent times. My father and grandfather both died a month apart in the summer of 1994, shortly after we moved out of the projects. And due to some rather moronic decisions on my part, I spent two months in Lake County Juvenile Center. Things finally settled down when my mom and her new boyfriend moved us to a small farming community called Kouts, about an hour away from the ghettos that had been steadily dragging me through the gutter towards the sewer. This new town and school introduced a feeling of stability in my life that let my love of reading and writing blossom.

The story began as another of my patented rip-offs. This time a zombie story, which came to life after a weekend spent watching Romero's classics. My story took place in my school rather than a shopping mall, and as always starred myself. The first version was my longest effort of any kind, thirteen pages, but something was different. It felt incomplete. For the first time I started a second draft and came up with thirty-two pages of cramped handwriting.

It still wasn't done, but something more important came up: summer vacation. The story stayed in the back of my mind and my junior year of high school I started the third draft, this time on one of the old Apple computers in my library. I was a library aide during third period and would spend my free time writing, often skipping lunch to keep in the groove. By the end of the school year the story had grown to 80 pages, but I still wasn't done.

My home life jumped back in and created a few problems, but also opportunity. Due to a dispute with my mother's boyfriend, forever known as Dickhead in my mind, I moved out of my house and in with a friend whose mother had a spare bedroom. She also had an old computer, and wondered if I'd mind having it in my room. I was ecstatic, and shortly after began work on my fourth draft.

A year and a half later I had a full-blown novel on my hands, 235 pages of zombie goodness. The clumsy, awkward prose of the earlier versions was replaced by a more mature—but still somewhat juvenile—style of writing. I had even replaced myself and my friends with original characters. As I neared completion I couldn't contain my excitement. I was 18 and about a finish my first novel!

And then disaster.

After a blowup with my friend, it was time to move. In a fit of apathetic anger I saved my story to a floppy disk and tossed it in a box full of the assorted junk I had collected over the years. Seashells from the Atlantic Ocean, a few shot glasses from various vacation trips, old notebooks, love letters from girlfriends, a pocket watch, and tragically, a large magnet in the shape of Kenny from *South Park*. I then deleted the story off the computer and despite an intuitive feeling inside me screaming to stop, I emptied the Recycle Bin. I took my belongings and left, ignorant of what I had just unintentionally done.

Needless to say, when I discovered that the disk was empty, I was devastated. Almost four years of work down the drain. All that remained were eighty pages of sloppy writing from the third draft. It's hard to describe the feeling of heartbreak and hopelessness. To have worked so hard and been so proud of what I had and to know those years of work had disappeared in an instant. Devastated is too weak a word. I felt my whole world collapsing. For years I had believed, with perhaps too much fervor, that this book was my ticket to something better. Fame and fortune! Maybe it was better that I lost the book, rather than facing the disappointment of rejection. I don't know.

What I do know is I didn't write another word for myself for four years. I couldn't. Occasionally I would sit at my computer and type the first line of the story, a line I knew by heart just as I knew the entire story: *"Kazuo Astor stared into the setting sun and wondered how much longer he had to live."*

I would get that far, but no further. Never any further. It was like my creative flow had dried up or been dammed. Not even a trickle would come through, until I decided to register for the creative writing class my sophomore year at Indiana State University. Only then did the creative juices start flowing again and I found I could write. I still couldn't face the prospect of starting the novel, but short stories began to come in spades. I was writing again, and it was great.

Those creative writing classes also led to my membership in the creative writing group, Arion. Two years later I was the president of the group and editor-in-chief of the yearly journal, *The Tonic*. It was that work which eventually led to this book you're now holding in your hands. I love writing, but I also love being able to provide a conduit for others to display their talent.

This is not the book I have dreamed of publishing since I was a sixteen-year-old furiously scribbling in my notebook, and I'm okay with that. This is a book I'm proud of, a book that contains the works of twenty very talented individuals.

The stories and poems in this collection can't be nailed down to one specific category. There is a little something for everyone. Comedy, drama, thriller, mystery, even a little yarn about zombies. The only connecting thread is that every one of the authors within this collection lives or have lived in the state of Indiana, hence the title. Much like the collection of people living in the state and this country, it's a hodgepodge. A melting pot.

I have greatly enjoyed bringing this anthology to life and being able to present it to the world. I hope you enjoy it half as much.

Will the Circle Be Unbroken?

Jared Yates Sexton

When the beer ran out the Indy game was just in the second quarter and neither Hank or me were ready to call it quits on drinking. It was Sunday though, God's day, and all the liquor stores were closed and Kroger's put out signs saying the State of Indiana prohibited sale.

Hank watched another draw play go nowhere and drained the last drop from the last can. He said, "There's gotta be something we can do."

But there wasn't anything really. Grass had dried out in the county and I'd already told Hank I was done huffing now that I had a little girl to look after. We tried next door but Taylor was out of town. His wife answered and said she wasn't comfortable handing out any of the beers he kept in his garage.

By the time the game went to the half we were both desperate. Hank got shaky without a beer in his hand and I had too much on my mind not to drink. See, back then Audrey and me were fussing all the time and it looked like any day might be our last. I tried to talk to her about it, to sit her down and try and get to the root of our problems, but she'd already got to that point of roughness women tend to get to when their love is running dry.

One night I cornered her in the bedroom after she'd gotten out of the shower. She had a towel tied around herself and was brushing her hair in the mirror in our bedroom. Watching her like that, running that brush through her long brown hair and knowing she'd rather die than give me some attention, I got to feeling sick to my stomach. I couldn't hold it back anymore.

I said, "Why've you gone so cold?"

She wouldn't even look at me when she said she didn't know. She just kept her eyes on her reflection. I tried to ask again, but all she'd say was something about needing to see her friend Peggy.

It didn't matter what she said, I knew something was weighing on her.

As for the beer, Hank finally got on the horn and rung up his wife's cousin Gill. Gill, he told me, was a guy who was good at getting things.

I asked why he didn't just call him earlier.

"Bad blood," Hank said.

We both had a decent buzz going at that point so we took the back roads across town. Hank about shit when we whipped by an officer parked out at the FOP. Even after we passed him it took Hank a good couple of minutes to quit checking his mirrors and sit up straight in his seat.

Aside from the cop the day was just about perfect. Fall was pushing in and I could hear every bird in every tree in the forest around us. I clicked on the radio and found a station playing old church hymnals. Usually I would've flipped right past, but something about all those voices singing as one really hit me right. I turned up the volume and let those good Christian people sing about forgiveness and charity while Hank searched through his ashtray for a couple of half-spent roaches. He fished one out and we passed it around. Pretty soon we were both feeling about ten times better than we did whenever we ran out of beer.

On the way though, a little farther down the road, I started thinking about Audrey again and it was all I could do to hold onto any kind of hope. It seemed like she'd already written us off and would rather have spent time with Peggy than me.

Peggy was this woman who'd moved in across the street. Her husband Neal bowled and we played leagues together while the girls got thick as thieves. She was nice enough, I guess, but I got the real feeling she liked to talk bad about me to Audrey. Every time I got good and boozed up she'd shake her head and whisper something in my lady's ear. Then the two of them would take turns shaking their head and Audrey would be awful sore to me the rest of the night.

'For too long Hank and me pulled into a blind drive out by the Gun Club. At the end of the drive was a little brown house surrounded by pink rose bushes. There were all kinds of lawnmowers, riders and pushers and the old ones without engines, sitting out in the yard. Wild grass was growing up and over their wheels. Off to the side was a new-looking aluminum garage with a bunch of street signs bolted to the walls.

"There he is," Hank said. I looked over and saw a guy walking out without a shirt on. His chest and arms looked sunburned all to hell and he had long blonde hair tied up into a ponytail. I thought maybe I'd seen him out in town somewhere, but I couldn't quite place the face.

The guy pulled Hank into a bear hug as soon he stepped out of the truck. "Henry Jack," he said, thumping Hank on the back. "You don't come round near enough," he said. "You know that?"

"Sure thing," Hank said. "Gill, Jerry. Jerry, Gill."

"Howdy," I said.

Gill looked at me like he held some kind of grudge. I thought, right then, that he might come at me and my whole body went tight. Instead, he spit on the ground and rubbed it in the dirt with the toe of his boot. "You boys lookin' for some party supplies?" he said.

In the garage Gill had a broken down combine wedged into a corner and a couple of old pickups parked every which way next to the big machine. Tools laid around in greasy piles on the concrete floor. On the other side of the garage, where the three of us were sitting, were two couches that reeked of mold and a small refrigerator he used as a coffee table. There was a dusty bag of pills on top.

"Make yourself at home," Gill said, flopping down on one of the couches. Hank and me grabbed us a seat on the other one. "Don't ya'll worry either," Gill said, "Samantha took the kids to Terre Haute to buy some school clothes, so there ain't gonna be anybody runnin' in or botherin' our shit."

Hank and me sat there while Gill dug into the little refrigerator and pulled out a couple sixers of Pabst. When he handed me one I could feel how cold they were, like they were just about ready to freeze solid. That's how I liked my beer best. I popped one open and took me a healthy drink. It was like ice.

"Let me tell you somethin'," Gill said. He handed Hank a handful of pills from the dusty bag and offered me some too. I was feeling guilty, being a father and all, so I said no thanks. Gill looked hurt for a second there, but then he went right on talking. "This no sellin' booze on Sunday shit don't make any sense. And bitching about it don't do any good either. I've been into town tryin' to buy some brews on a Sunday before. I stomp and shout but it ain't like they're just goin' to break down and sell you some."

Next to me Hank was slurping from his beer and popping a pill every now and then. "I know it," he said.

Gill kicked his feet up on the refrigerator and swirled his own beer around in its can. "And this doesn't have anything to do with Jesus neither." He nodded and brought the can up to his mouth like he was going to take a drink, but then got back to jawing. "There ain't no passage in the Bible of anyone sayin' drinkin' is bad or that someone shouldn't be able to find some Pabst on a Sunday. Try and find me that in the King James and you'll be lookin' for awhile."

"Amen," Hank said.

"Shit," Gill said after a couple of seconds.

We all finished off a beer and cracked open another. Hank talked Gill into getting out a black and white set and turning on the game. The third quarter was coming to an end and the Colts were down by a touchdown and a field goal. The three of us huddled around the TV and sucked down that beer as fast as we could. I got enough in my belly at that point to start feeling real good. I was watching that game and thinking about how green that grass probably was in person and how those boys out on the field were putting their everything into every play. Sitting around there with Hank and Gill I almost forgot about all the bad feelings I'd been having about Audrey.

Right before the fourth quarter the game went to a commercial and Hank got up to take a piss. The commercial was for carbon monoxide detectors. A happy family was sitting down to eat supper at the kitchen table and the mom was passing around a bowl of mashed potatoes and a big jug full of lemonade. Everything was really nice and beautiful until a serious-sounding voice spoke and said that carbon monoxide was slowly killing everyone in the house. The voice said no one knew it, but the gas was spreading. It said all it took to find out if carbon monoxide was a problem in your home was a detector you could get for twenty dollars or so.

I was focusing on that commercial, or rather that family at the table. They looked so happy, the dad wearing a tie and helping his little daughter spoon some peas off her plate. The mom kept reaching over and adjusting the bib around her baby son's neck. I could almost see that gas sneaking down into their lungs and killing off their cells one by one. Somehow I could already see them old and withered, suffocating and not knowing why.

For some reason that got me wondering about my daughter Jasmine. Audrey had dropped her off at her folks so she could go run some errands. I didn't know what kind of errands a person could run on a Sunday, but I was starting to worry about the whole deal. Jasmine was getting a little older and starting to ask questions.

"Where's Mom?" she'd say. "Where's Mom?"

Half the time I didn't know what to say. I had to shrug and hope someday I'd have an answer too.

Gill tossed the magazine at me. It landed in my lap and it took me a little bit to figure out what'd happened. When I picked it up I could see it was a cheap porno mag turned to a centerfold of a blonde-haired woman. She didn't have a lick of anything on and there was another girl, this one with brown hair, down by her business. The brown haired girl had her tongue curled out like a snake's. Both of them looked like they were in ecstasy.

"Jerry," Gill said. "You like eatin' pussy?"

I looked at the centerfold again and could barely take my eyes off that blonde's business. It was pink and looked so close and real I thought I could reach out and touch it. "Yeah," I said.

"Fuckin' A," Gill said. "I tell almost everyone I meet. I think I like eatin' pussy more than just about anything else in this whole goddamn world."

My attention moved to the brunette down between the other girl's thighs. I kept going back over her tongue and the look pasted on her face. She looked more excited than anyone I'd ever seen getting ready to do anything. I thought it was almost a perfect picture in how well it caught her in that moment. I believed, I mean I really believed that that woman was ready to dive in at any second.

Hank came back and got himself an eye full. "Jesus Christ," he said. He nudged me with his elbow and said, to himself I think, "Jesus Christ" again.

"There's just somethin' about it," Gill said. He leaned back in the cushions and scratched his chest and stomach. His skin was glowing red at that point and it was like his whole body was giving off some kind of heat. "It's like shovin' your face into a birthday cake," he said. "Just gettin' down there and gettin' into the good stuff."

I stared at that picture until it became just a big pink blur. Then I'd look again and zero in on their faces. They looked like any number of women I'd met before, any number I'd bedded. They didn't look a thing like Audrey, but sitting there and looking at them made me start thinking about her somehow. I thought about her lying down on top of our sheets and getting in the same state as that blonde. I kept trying to picture myself down there, my tongue hanging out of my mouth like an old dog's, but for some reason I couldn't do it. Whenever I tried all I could ever do was see Peggy, our neighbor and Neal's wife.

"Shit," Gill said. He polished off another beer and crushed the can. The trash was a few feet away and he tossed the beer can toward it like he was shooting a basketball. It hit the side and clanged down to the floor. "You know, my girl Sam's a handful. Sometimes she gets stuck on something so bad nothin' will get her off it. Like last month she started making these photo albums. Started going through all these boxes and boxes of pictures her mom left her. Stuff from as far back as Dubya Dubya Two, and she got it in her head she was going to get all this shit organized and taped to a page."

Hank tried to yank the magazine away but I had a good grip on it and kept hold. I needed to look at it some more.

"So anyway," Gill said, "I took her into town and we bought all kinds of stuff. Albums and glue and special scissors." He grabbed a beer from the fridge and popped the top. "Pair of scissors cost me twenty-five goddamn dollars. Can you believe that? A pair of goddamn scissors."

"Goddamn," Hank said. He reached across to the bag and got him another fistful of pills.

Gill laughed. "Exactly," he said. "That's exactly what I said. Goddamn. And we get back here, and for a couple of days she does it. She gets all these pictures out and gets them in order. And I'll be damned if she doesn't get a half of an album done up before she tosses all that shit in the closet and says the hell with it."

I remembered all the times I'd laid Audrey down on our bed or across the backseat of our car and how she'd always said no whenever I started to go down. She never wanted me anywhere near that place. She'd get real fussy and start kicking a little. Grabbing at my hair and yanking me up.

"I took her aside and gave her a piece of mind," Gill said. "You'd better believe it. We fought and carried on up and down the house all night. But the point was we couldn't afford pissin' away money like that on every little thing that caught her eye."

By then I wasn't even looking at the magazine anymore. My mind was on Audrey and Peggy. I tried to remember how they were when they were together. How sometimes they hugged or kissed each other on the cheek. I thought of a couple of times where they'd said goodbye for an extra long time.

"But let me tell you," Gill said. "That woman's got the finest pussy God ever put on this green Earth. That thing alone makes me believe in scripture and good will and all that Sunday morning shit."

At that point I couldn't help but picture them in Peggy and Neal's living room, on the couch in front of the TV I'd helped Neal carry in. There was a shelf above the set that held all the trophies we'd won. The City Tourney, State Finals, even the Friday Night Charity Bowl where we had a combined five hundred pins. The two of them, Audrey and Peggy, were sprawled across the cushions. It was a green couch with blue flowers printed all over and it made their bodies look whiter. My Audrey was on her back with her legs open like some storm shutters. Her body was flushed and covered in sweat. Peggy, with a mop of curly blonde hair, was down there eyeing her up real good. Her pink, pink tongue was out and ready.

Pretty soon I got to feeling sick again and told Hank I wanted to take off. Gill gave us another sixer apiece and we got in the truck and headed down the road. The day was still just as pretty, but I couldn't focus on any birds or trees or anything else for that matter.

Hank got to whistling and turned on the radio again. That choir from earlier popped on and started singing out to the Lord, saying the circle would be unbroken and all that. That there was a better home a-waitin'. I grabbed another Pabst off the ring and leaned my head way out the window to try and get a good taste of the air. No doubt there was something waiting, but I couldn't for the life of me figure what that something was.

While you were sleeping

Sarah Long

I was lying
in a cold bath
shocked
like a boiled tomato
in a bowl of
iced water.

Fuzz Bomb

Sarah Long

Walks down the street
A city street
Sifting through
The spectrum of maple leaves
With his topsiders
That his wife coordinated with
His brown corduroys
And his sepia tone western-style dress shirt.
Light refracts off of the pearl buttons,
Spreads across his milky pupils
Giving warmth to the blind man
With a tired life,
Delicate and freckled hands,
And a brain stuffed with nuggets
Of petrified wisdom.

I once resented this man,
My uncle,
Loathed his sculptured opinion
Displayed to me
Like store-front Christmas propaganda,
Ridiculous philosophies
About keeping up with the Joneses
Or going to the court house

To change his family's last name
Meanwhile, honing
A Cheshire grin
And scratching his manliness
That is fashionably
Quarantined by a white
Fruit-of the-Loom contemporary cod piece.

When I see him going for a stroll, I wince.
I hear the metronomic tick of his cane
On the broken sidewalk.
I am convinced that he will never be humble
And, for the first time,
I would like to hold his hand when he crosses the street
And looks both ways for him;
But the light is green and I have other places to be.
Apparently, he does too.

The Summer of Zucchini

Sarah Long

Three weeks ago mom made zucchini bread.
I watched the spiced sludge slosh
in a plastic mixing bowl.
She told me that raisins create magic
then she told me that
she's finding it hard to breathe with
a pair of arms wrapped around her chest
in a Heimlich position.

Two weeks ago
mom's chest was cracked open
and someone else reached inside
to do the work for her; but
she was still obliged to feel the pain.

My aunt made zucchini cakes the following day
in a surrogate oven; my mother's heat did the job.

I was given a zucchini
at the bar last Saturday night.
I felt like a real woman
because a recipe gravitated above
my head for five days afterwards.

That week during a spirituality seminar
I decided to pitch in for a potluck lunch.
I made zucchini muffins with cream cheese icing.
Magic.

I thought about this summer
and its affection for zucchini when:
I broke open the stubborn green fruit,
the respirator was yanked out of my mom's throat,
I pulled a bunch of plastic bags out from under
the kitchen sink,
handed them to my father to use for garbage bags.

Those bags,
How long will it take
to fill them all with trash?
Will it be in synchronization with
mom's life expectancy or
the zucchini mush that is being
preserved in the freezer?

Or
will it be a race?
To test human capability,
to measure wasteful tendencies,
to dictate happiness
through full bellies
stuffed with spiced summer vegetables?

Zucchini served as a security blanket
to me this summer.
I bit into the spongy surface
while mom's body staved off death.

Rogues

Nathan Jones

She was groggy every homogenous morning that summer after seventh grade. This one was no different. Fate wasn't on her mind. It might never be. Life's life. Home's home. No big deal. Kris turned on the faucet, a small steady stream. Not wanting to wake her family, she let water slowly fill the jug full of ice cubes, climbed up on a chair pulled over from the table. She got a small lunch cooler down from the top of the refrigerator and filled it with plastic baggies. Her mom had left two bologna sandwiches, a stick of string cheese, and a twenty-ounce bottle of pop for her in the fridge. These all went in the cooler. Kris also grabbed a package of Cheetos and the bag of grapes and blueberries she had left in the freezer overnight. By the time her lunch was packed, the jug of water was almost full. She turned off the faucet. She went into the mud-room and pulled on her filthy tennis shoes. Pieces of dried mud broke apart under her socks. The dust found its way inside the clean socks and between her already hot toes. She pawed through a pile of laundry on top of the drier and pulled out a faded blue sweatshirt, her favorite, with all the names from her brother's 1986 varsity squad screen-printed in two red rows on the back. She grabbed her work gloves, too. Moving into the morning, she was careful not to let the screen door slam.

The sun was barely over the horizon as Kris moved her ten-speed out of the detached garage. She put the lunch cooler on one side of the handle bars and her jug of water on the other side. She stamped her feet to get some of the dried mud loose from the tread of her shoes. Then she got on her bike, an old pink hand-me-down Huffy, and started to ride.

It was only 5:00 in the morning and quite cool, even for the middle of June. She was barely awake and let the bike work for her—riding with no hands on the handle bars. Rebalancing if needed, she glided over the street and listened to the weight of ice cubes shifting inside the jug. A light breeze moved over bare skin on her legs. She took a pony tail holder off of her wrist, held it in her mouth, and ran her fingers through her hair. She pulled her hair up as she rode. It was about a ten minute ride to the courthouse.

A few other kids were there—sitting on the peaked cement coping, eating donuts from the bakery. Two of the boys were rough-housing, but most of the kids were immobile and quiet. Kris didn't bother to acknowledge anyone and no one bothered to acknowledge her. It was early and they had all day to talk. She locked her bike up with the others and set her jug of ice water and her lunch cooler down on the courthouse lawn near some of her friends.

"Want anything?" She tilted her head towards the bakery.

One girl, Regina, shook her head and fell backwards onto the lawn, yawning, covering her face with her arm. Their other friend, Melanie, held up her half-eaten nut-roll, indicating she'd already been to the bakery and back. Kris crossed the street and walked into the bakery. Old farmers sat silent with their steaming coffee. She got an apple fritter and a large Styrofoam cup full of milk. The bakery used really thin straws. Kris loved drinking milk from the metal dispenser through the bakery's really thin straws.

She returned to the coping and sat between Melanie and Regina. Melanie reached for the milk and took a sip without comment. Regina still kept her arm over her face and tried to sleep.

If she was paying attention, there he was. Kyle walked up the side street to an intersection that laid flat under traffic lights, as if a road might matter. He looked both ways out of habit but walked into the road without hesitation. Not many cars moving this early. One pick-up parked in front of the bakery. He peeled a hardboiled egg, threw pieces of shell in the street. Didn't really look for her either.

As the kids assembled, more and more bikes were locked up at the bike racks, and more and more noise was made: clattering of plastic coolers against the concrete coping, soles of shoes scraping against edges of the curb and the steps leading to the courthouse, boys pushing, shoving, and jumping over each other from the lawn to the sidewalk and from the sidewalk to the street. The boys, all in dirty old clothes, started bothering the girls, slapping sunburn-blistered shoulders. One boy stepped on Regina's ponytail that was lying across the grass hoping that she would sit up and it would pull her hair. But she ignored him, lay still, and he went away.

At 5:30, a bus pulled up to the courthouse. It was an old school bus painted tan with the company name and logo on the side. Underneath the logo "Hybridizing Seed Corn since 1973" was carefully articulated in green paint. The kids stood up, gathered their sweatshirts and lunch coolers, and lined up. The boys pushed each other out of line and ran around the girls, swooping in and out of the line like barn swallows. The girls stood in close proximity to each other, shuffling their feet, looking around, telling the boys to quit it, waiting until it was their turn to step up onto the bus.

The steps and the aisle of the bus were caked with the season's mud. It dried into a layer about three inches thick and made walking on the bus more difficult than usual. The windows were smeared with mud that boys had wiped in zealous professions of love, which had then been rubbed off by the girls. Kris and Regina sat down in one seat and Melanie sat in the seat in front of them. The boy that liked Melanie sat down next to her, and his buddies giggled and smacked the top of his head as they filed past him into the rear of the bus.

Kris leaned her head on the window and waited for motion.

The bus moved through town. Small towns seem bigger early in the morning. Kris looked out the window as they passed the ice cream stand by the river, passed the statue of General Milroy in a park, his park, passed the judge's house, passed the Pizza King, passed the elementary school, passed the grocery store, passed the Catholic college and out onto the country highway that connected the remote town to the interstate.

After the bus lurched along between freshly painted yellow and white lines for twenty minutes, it pulled onto a country road. The road was unmarked, paved only the first mile. Then its surface switched to gravel. The bus, with some windows always stuck down, soon filled with a cloud of limestone dust. The kids barely noticed.

Arriving at the edge of a particular field, the bus slowed and eased off the road into a ditch. Mr. Allen, their supervisor who wore the same old ball cap every day, sat in a pick-up truck, waiting for them. As the bus pulled up he got out of his truck, spit, rolled his head in a slow circle, grabbed a clip board and got on the bus.

"Listen up. We're going to rogue the Elijah fields this morning, and then walk beans after lunch. It's supposed to storm later on. So we're going to walk these fields twice, not three times, this morning. We'll double back next week. Lunch will be pushed up so we can get over to those beans as early as possible. Now hustle up."

The kids stood up and started moving forward.

"Wait. A point of business. I need to see Thompson." Mr. Allen looked down at his clipboard. "Jason Thompson about your W-2. Jason?"

Jason Thompson was the boy who had a crush on Melanie. He got up and followed Mr. Allen off the bus and over to the pick-up. Jason listened to Mr. Allen's instructions and then worked his way through the form on another clipboard. Melanie kept an eye on him while she re-tied her shoes with double knots.

The kids left their coolers and water jugs under seats that would make shade soon and filed off the bus. The bus, in order to be off the thin gravel road, leaned precariously over the ditch. But the kids just adapted. They jumped down into the tall grass of the ditch that the bus leaned into and each crawled up the other side, scrambling, pulling at tall weeds to help their ascent. They followed each other over to the bed of the pick-up and grabbed shovels.

The shovels had wooden handles with their blades cut straight across and filed sharp. The kids pulled black trash bags out of a huge cardboard box and began biting them at the seams, creating holes for their heads and arms. Then the kids, dressed in black trash bags, splayed out along the rows of corn.

Kris, Regina, and Melanie moved early morning silent with the rest. Kris pulled on her mud-caked gloves. Regina carried her shovel across the back of her shoulders and draped her arms over either side of the handle. Melanie craned her neck every few steps, looking back toward Jason. He was talking to Mr. Allen. Both families had hogs. She knew the topic. Jason's family had recently hired a lawyer after a complaint had been filed by their new neighbor regarding the county's mandatory separation distance. The previous neighbors had signed an exemption waiver. But it was true that Jason's father's operation had expanded a great deal since that time. Jason discussed it, repeating his father's opinion almost verbatim to the man in the ball cap. Melanie watched him. She carried two shovels with good sharp blades.

The girls fell into the line-up—a kid to every male row of corn. Regina, Kris, and Melanie took their positions at the end of a row. "Hey! Scoot down. Scoot down one. Jason's coming."

Kris's hair loosened in its ponytail. It never mattered how tightly she pulled it—it always came loose. She pushed a strand behind her ear, staked her shovel three inches into the uneven loam, and put her foot up on one side. Kris waited ready, wearing the trash bag and leaning her chin on her arm. She steadied the handle of her planted shovel.

The sun rose imperceptibly but had not yet conquered the tree line.

Melanie watched Jason hand the clipboard back to Mr. Allen. She had already gotten him a trash bag and a shovel. She motioned for him to join her and her friends. His buddies hollered at him from down the line—he waved them off and jogged towards Melanie. She handed him the trash bag first. He carefully tore a v-shape from the center of the trash bag base. Then he turned the bag and carefully tore a half-circle on each side of the bag. He pulled the bag over his head. He adjusted it to his liking and then took the shovel from Melanie.

As soon as Jason was ready, Mr. Allen shouted. "Okay. Down and back."

The kids moved into the corn.

Kris stepped into the rows. She walked to the left of the male row and scanned it and the four female rows to her right. The ground was still wet under a thin layer of dried topsoil so her feet sank with each step. The furrows between the rows of corn made her footing unsure. She walked carefully and watched for clods of dirt and unexpected dips, which could complicate her path. But her eyes scanned her rows. The corn was about four feet tall and laden with morning dew. Leaves unloaded the water caught under millions of hair-holds onto her waist, thighs, shins, and ankles. The trash-bag kept her sweatshirt dry, but she was chilled. The water collected around the edge of the trash-bag and soaked her old jean shorts. After her shorts were saturated, the water began to run down. Her sneakers filled with water. Cases of mud formed around her shoes. The weight and girth of the mud made her footing even more unsteady, but she was used to these mornings in the fields.

She scanned her rows. There. She raised the shovel handle and pulled her arm back. She plunged the shovel down quickly, slicing through the corn stalk she had singled out. She did not stop but always worked in motion, walking up the row, scanning her territory, slicing down any aberrant plants.

A rogue was anything out of the ordinary. The instructions were to cut down any plant that was in any way different from the others. If a stalk was too thick, cut it down. If a stalk was too dark green, cut it down. If a stalk was too insipid looking or yellow, cut it down. If a stalk was too tall, cut it down. Because in June the plants were really growing, really showing their spurt.

The row of kids moved steadily through the field, all alerted to variation. They began to really wake-up to the rustle of trash bags and leaves, to the sound of intermittent slicing, to the movement of cool wind drying the acres.

Regina shouted over to Jason. "What'd he say about your W-2?"

Jason sliced through a thick green stalk and squinted, looking toward Regina. She was to the East of him. "My Dad had signed it, but they needed me to sign it too. I guess I remembered my Dad telling me to sign it, but I didn't have a pen on the bus so I just turned it in."

Regina scraped mud from her shoes onto a rock in her row. "Yeah. You weren't here the first week. Where were you?"

"I was in North Carolina. My family always goes to the beach that first week out of school."

Kris shouted over to Melanie. "How do you like that, Mel? When we were all out here picking up rocks, your boyfriend was getting a tan on the beach."

Melanie laughed, moving back towards her male row after slicing down a double-female stalk. "Your tan looks better than his does. He just turns all red."

Regina turned to Kris. "Plus, Krissy, don't forget that he brought her back that pretty dolphin necklace." Regina widened her eyes and tried not to laugh. Both Kris and Regina thought the necklace was ugly. It was a pewter dolphin attached to a tiny blue marble, which made it look like a dolphin jumping over the entire earth. The necklace itself was braided black leather. The girls knew Melanie thought it was ugly too, but she'd never admit it. She wore it every day.

Regina was jealous of Melanie, who had long curly auburn hair and a real boyfriend. Regina's hair was thin and straight and always went limp even if she curled it. Kris turned away from Regina's stare so that Melanie and Jason wouldn't perceive any commiseration.

To the East, the sun had finally risen above the tree line and was beginning to burn off the haze. The line of workers in the field moved steadily forward but also undulated. Each kid moved at roughly the same pace as those around him or her, but the row expanded and contracted and bulged out in places as Kris looked over at everyone in the line.

"Krissy! Hey. To your right. Not your left. Pay attention!"

Kris looked back over her shoulder. The foreman, a high school sophomore, sliced a thick stalk out of one of her female rows. "Sorry, Kyle. Thanks." She watched him move back and forth over about seven of the kids' rows. He was a little taller and could see the rogues from further away.

Regina saw Kris looking at Kyle. She screamed to Kyle, who was working his way back to the East. "Kyle, Krissy just wants you to follow right behind her. That's why she missed that obvious one. You know she likes you."

Melanie turned to Regina. "Shut up, Regina."

Kris stopped for a moment to pull off her gloves. She pulled the trash bag up so that she could tuck the gloves inside the back of her waistband.

Regina turned to Kris. "Come on, Krissy, he'll catch up. You don't have to wait for Kyle back there."

Jason joined his girlfriend in defense of Kris, "Regina, don't be like that."

Regina retorted. "Melanie, tell your stupid boyfriend to shut-up."

None of the kids talked to each other for a while. They listened to the other voices drifting over the morning and concentrated on their rows.

Most fields were a mile long. The motion through the fields was slow, but eventually they reached the other side. When Kris, Regina, Jason, and Melanie came to the end of their rows, other kids were already finished and were sitting down on their shovels or using the shovel blades to scrape mud from their shoes.

When all the kids were out of the rows and all the foremen were out of the rows, and Mr. Allen had walked back and forth, counting the kids twice, he signaled with an arm over his head and all the kids turned around and moved into the rows again.

Back down the same rows.

Stepping over rocks and this time over cut down rogues too.

There were always more aberrations in walking back—seen from a different perspective, or overlooked the first time in pursuing another. Strange how there was just as much work to do walking back as there was walking down.

When they got back to the original side of the field, it was getting warmer. The dew had dried and the trash bags were humid inside and dry on the outside. The bags were piled into the back of the truck. Kris took off her sweatshirt and tied it around her waist as they walked in a long line down to the next section of the field. Down and back again. And then they took a water break. Someone had fallen over when a pheasant flew up out of his row and right over his head. He had hit his knee on a piece of drainage tile which had made its way to the surface during the Spring thaw when the fields were disked. The kids all watched Mr. Allen pouring peroxide over the scrape and listened to the kid tell how shocked both he and the pheasant had been. They laughed and sipped water that was too cold on their teeth.

Wax-covered paper cups piled up in the back of the pick-up truck on top of the trash bags. One kid showed Mr. Allen how a screw had come out of the shovel he was using and that it was too loose to be effective. Mr. Allen put the faulty shovel in the cab of the truck and indicated that the kid should get another shovel with a nod of his head toward the bed of the truck. The kids reacted to the same nod and dispersed with their shovels back toward the rows. It was their third section of the morning. They waited while Mr. Allen counted all of them by walking down and back along the whole row of kids. Kris looked at the blisters on her palms. In another week, they'd be calluses. Melanie looked down at the mud-encrusted double-knots she had tied in the morning, drying into impenetrable shards of concrete.

Jason spoke to Melanie for a moment and then moved ahead to rejoin his buddies. As soon as he was out of earshot Regina said, "Why do you even wear that necklace? It's atrocious."

Melanie turned to Regina. "Because he gave it to me. And because he was thinking of me when we were apart."

Regina chewed at some dirt under her thumbnail and spit it out. "He wasn't thinking very hard. And if he knew you at all, he'd know better than to think about you with that ugly ass necklace."

Kris intervened. "Shut-up, Regina. I don't see your boyfriend bringing you any jewelry from anywhere."

Regina was going with an older boy. He was contracting that summer. He was responsible for fifteen fields of corn and had five other high school guys working them with him. "That's because he doesn't go anywhere. He's always working. He's only got five guys in his crew this summer and they've got a ton of acres. He's making lots of money this summer. He's saving up."

"To do what? Go drinking with his buddies at that stupid abandoned gas station? When has he ever taken you anywhere since he got his license?" Melanie raised her voice slightly. It was getting hot out.

The girls moved into the field when Mr. Allen finally shouted for them to start.

Regina thought as they worked for almost thirty yards. "He took me to the movies."

Melanie laughed. "That doesn't count. His mom sent you to babysit his little sister, because she knew she couldn't trust her own son when she had to work. You guys saw a cartoon."

"Well we made out even if it was a cartoon."

Kris said, "You made out in front of his little sister? That's trashy, Regina."

"You're one to talk, Krissy. And anyway she fell asleep."

The girls walked and talked, raising up their shovels and bringing them down hard through the rogues—killing them off.

It was important work. Hybridizing seed corn is complex. The male rows had certain attributes that would be good for the next year's corn. And the female rows had certain attributes that would be good for the next year's corn. But male or female, any strange stalks couldn't be allowed to reproduce. Every plant had to be similar so that yields would be high. The next year's corn had to fit the machinery if the yields were to be high—uniformity helped. The girls knew it. It's why they got paid.

In May, they got paid to pick up rocks. In June, they got paid to rogue. In July, they would detassel, and by August there was no more work to do. They would be back in school and let quiet time work instead, letting wind carry the pollen to the female rows. Then all the male rows would be cut down, and Fall would move into the ripening fields. November, if dry enough, would keep its neck down low in its collar. Once harvested the seed moved in red trucks to the drying elevator, and the female rows were plowed under.

The girls walked down their rows as cumulus clouds formed on the horizon. The corn leaves began to curl up. The foremen started shouting to each other and then to their crews to work a little faster.

The girls picked up their pace. When they got to the end of the row, each foreman waited until his seven kids were out of the field, counted them and then sent them right back up the rows as Mr. Allen had instructed them. The girls worked hard, scanning the rows, cutting down rogues, and walking fast. The corn leaves, dry now, sliced their shins, thighs, and arms and left hundreds of tiny cuts, like paper cuts, on their skin. Their foreman Kyle moved behind them, encouraging them to keep up the pace and get back to the bus for lunch.

In the bus, the girls found their way back to their seats. Jason sat down next to Melanie and put his arm around her. She turned her head and spoke to him. No one else heard the conversation. Kris drank from her jug of water, still cold from all the morning's ice cubes. Regina let her ponytail drape over the back of the seat so that it was in the lap of the boy behind her.

"Get your nasty hair off me, Regina."

"Shut up. I'm just trying to rest for a minute."

"Well put your hair on your side of the seat."

"Fine. Whatever." Regina tossed her head and after brushing her hair across his lap several times pulled her ponytail back onto her side of the seat.

The bus took them to a farm house near the fields they would work in the afternoon. The driver parked it under the shade of some trees by a pole barn and the kids unloaded themselves with their lunch coolers. They spread out over the front lawn of the farm house, and sat down to eat. There was a row of portable toilets and a huge sycamore tree. The lawn was perfectly maintained. Geraniums grew in a plastic goose.

Melanie, Kris, Regina, and Jason sat in the shade of the sycamore. Jason started on a smashed peanut butter and jelly sandwich. Regina ate a packaged cupcake. Melanie opened a tiny Tupperware container full of potato salad.

Kris pulled a wet washcloth out of a baggie. She wiped her face and then her hands with it. It cooled her down. Then she handed it to Regina whose hand was out. "You think of everything, Krissy. That's why I love you." Regina passed the washcloth to Melanie who ran it over the back of her neck and then Jason's neck.

"Thanks." Kris pulled out her frozen blueberries and grapes. She sucked on a frozen grape and pressed it against the roof of her mouth. Kyle came up and sprawled out near them. "It's supposed to rain. Mr. Allen wants us to walk those drill beans though. Because if the field really gets wet again we won't be able to get in it for two weeks and that pig weed and mustard will have really taken hold by then. So unless you hear thunder we're not going home until three, rain or no rain."

Regina looked at him. "Are you serious? He can't do that."

"Well that's why we're not rogueing this afternoon. No shovels to attract the lightening. And he won't keep us out there if it's really pouring. But if it's just sprinkling he wants to get that field done."

Kris looked at Kyle but kept eating her lunch. She listened to everything he said and started on her string cheese. She wanted to say something. "You want my Cheetos, Kyle?"

"Sure. You're not gonna eat them?"

"I always bring too much." She handed him the bag.

"Thanks." He rolled over and lay down on his back looking up into the sycamore tree. Then he shifted and propped his head up on her outstretched ankle. "You don't mind do you?"

"You're fine." Kris pulled up a blade of grass and pulled it through her fingernails repeatedly.

Regina had been thinking since Melanie had confronted her. She said, "Kyle. What do those guys do at that old gas station anyway?"

Kyle laughed. "Not much. Drink beer. Light fireworks. Shoot road signs. Stupid shit."

Regina ran her fingers through Melanie's hair. "But like who goes there? Is it just guys?"

"Mostly. You checking up on your little boyfriend, Regina? Why don't you ask him what he does? Don't ask me to watch him for you."

"I'm not. He calls me every night. He tells me everything. I just wondered if girls go too." Regina started to braid Melanie's hair.

"Well once in a while. But I better never catch you up there. You're way too young."

"I'm only three years younger than you, Kyle."

"Well fourteen is still a whole lot different than seventeen."

Regina looked at Kris. "It sure is."

Kris shifted her ankle and Kyle pulled himself up onto his elbow.

Melanie said, "'Gina's boyfriend just turned sixteen. He thinks he's hot because he got his license and goes over there now. She's just worried he's running over there with some other girl from Tri-County or something."

"No. I've never seen him with a girl up there. He's younger than most of the guys so he just stands around looking stupid sipping on the one or two beers they give him. Nothin' crazy."

Jason, who was turning fifteen at the end of September, said, "My dad's already looking around for a truck for me. I'm saving this summer and next summer. Then we're going to split the price when I turn sixteen."

Kyle sat all the way up. "What are you looking for?"

"Black. Something small. S-10 maybe."

"What year?"

"Doesn't matter as long as it runs."

"That shouldn't set you back too much."

Regina dropped Melanie's braid, irritated by the guys talking to each other. "Kyle, why don't you find out how much longer we have for lunch from Mr. Allen?"

"Why, Regina? You already know. We've got like five minutes."

Kris got up and started to walk to the portable toilets. Melanie followed her and Regina did too after saying, "Whatever, Kyle. I'll ask him myself."

Mr. Allen had been inside the farm house eating his lunch with friends in their air conditioning. Right then he came out on the goose's side-porch holding a glass of lemonade and said, "Five minutes. Put your coolers on the bus. Get some water. Then line up from the driveway here to as far down the road as you can. I want each of you to stand five paces apart. That means when you get to the last person on the row, you stop and count five steps with your left foot, and then stop. Then the next person counts their five paces off you. You'll be spread out enough that we can cover this whole field in one shot—down and back. Pull everything growing that's not soybeans. Let's get to it." Mr. Allen turned to take his empty glass back inside the house. In another minute he was back outside with his clipboard, wearing his hat.

Kris came back to the sycamore shade from the portable toilets and looked for her cooler. Kyle shouted to her from inside the bus. "Krissy. Don't worry. I got it. I put it here on your seat."

She walked over to the bus. "Thanks, Kyle. Can you put this over there too?" She handed him her sweatshirt through the half open bus window and smiled.

Kyle held the sweatshirt. "Anything for you, little Krissy."

"Little? No more Cheetos for you."

Regina walked up behind her. "Let's go Kris. Kyle just needs to get over himself. And you need to get over him too."

Melanie hurried from behind, leaving Jason to find his friends. "Wait up, girls!"

The three girls, tan with sun-bleached arm hair, walked up the gravel road. Corn fields, soybean fields, the work was the same and the work was different every day. It was the same and it was different every season, every year. The workers were the same and the workers were different over time. Kris was first to the end of the line. She counted five paces and stopped. Regina walked on counting five paces out loud in a sing-song voice and stopped. And Melanie went on carefully counting three paces and then backing up to Regina again to start over and count five better paces so she would definitely come out right.

The girls waited for the signal and then walked into the fields. Bushy soybean leaves swirled around their thighs. Kyle came up behind the girls imitating Mr. Allen in a booming voice. "Drill beans are planted not in rows but in swirls; they're drilled into the soil. This kind of planting increases the yield per acre and minimizes the area available for weeds. But weeds still abound."

Kyle pushed Regina's shoulder almost hard enough to tip her over.

"Quit it, Kyle."

Kyle moved away from the girls and started working with Jason and his buddies.

The girls wore their gloves and pulled those tall prairie weeds all the way across the field. The clouds moved across the sky and shaded the girls from the sun. They laughed. They shouted. They bickered. They flirted with boys. They worked hard. And when the rain started, Mr. Allen, having planned well, had them out of the field and already lined up for the bus.

Regina ended up in the back of the bus with two other girls and six of the boys, looking at a toad that one kid had found in the bean field. Melanie and Jason leaned on each other and looked out the bus windows at the rain.

The big drops fell on the roof of the bus.

Kris felt mud drying against her skin. She looked at the seats and the floor and the insides of the bus windows where mud was drying to dirt. And she looked out where rain was turning dirt to mud. She leaned forward and opened her lunch cooler. She found the baggie with the dirty washcloth from lunch. It was still wet and cold. She used it on her raw weed-eaten legs. Since Regina had gone to the back of the bus, Kyle came and sat down next to Kris in her seat.

She looked at him and laid the folded washcloth down carefully on her left thigh. Kyle picked it up off her thigh. He rubbed it between his hands and pulled each finger through it. He folded it exactly the way she had folded it, and put it back on her thigh exactly where she had placed it. Then he took her right hand in both his hands. He traced the beds of her fingernails with his jagged nails. He turned her hand so it was open in his and traced her calluses with his index finger. Then he pulled her open palm up to his sunburned lips and kissed it—sort of. He ran her bent tan fingers over his jagged cracked lips, and then he let her hand fall, fingers entwined with his, onto the grubby seat between them, holding on. The bean leaves were even worse than the corn. Her shins and calves burned with small incisions made by edges of leaves.

The Gray Woman

Dalila Huerta

She rushes down the stairs, but her presence goes un noticed. The labyrinth of chairs, sugar packets, Styrofoam cups, and women remains oblivious to her worry-unceasing the swift inhalation of its food. Those twenty tables, devouring their second plates of homemade mush under flickering fluorescent lights, meet her only with the back of their coats. Her walk is haste, desperate, but she's nothing more than a ghost to all, a passing breeze that briefly disrupts their appointments with carbs and protein as some grains of rice fall victim to her draft.

She's invisible.

Her heavy parka, only shades darker than the blocked—cement walls, sucks her into the plain backdrop of a cold and dismal gray. I only notice her frantic eyes, a vivid green, her urgent look piercing my own like a cat ready to pounce. They're angry. Dazed. Hopeless. I can only offer the meager leftovers: a lone pork chop, dry and cold, with a spoonful of vegetables and a sprinkle of rice. She came too late. On my way home, I enjoy a hot dog bought on the street next to the soup kitchen. I doubt the street will bring much comfort to her.

Reno Sings the Blues

Jon Hueber

The waitress sat the pitcher on the table, spilling a splash up over the curved spout, and exchanged my dirty glass with a fresh one. I mouthed a thank you, which was ignored as she wormed her way through the crowd of people standing around the table. It was standing room only from this point on. The host barked something over the mic, but the words were drowned out in the noise of the people deep in their personal conversations.

The first contestant took the stage to a smattering of applause and launched into a tried and true bar-crowd favorite. Something by Kenny Chesney, or Travis Tritt, or some other boot-wearing shit kicker. The lyrics were projected in large print on the wall behind the stage allowing everyone in the bar to watch and read along. The sound whined with sharp feedback, but the contestant kept singing, his voice barely distinguishable over the noise. No one seemed to care and the when the song ended, the applause was minimal at best. The contestant melted into the sea of people and the host told a joke that no one got.

* * *

"I found a lump," I said. The voice on the other end of the phone was silent.

"You're gonna need to get it checked out," she said finally.

"I really can't afford to go to the doctor."

"It's not really up for debate."

"That's easy for you to say," I said. It was again met with silence. I could hear her breathing, thinking, carefully selecting her next words. I waited patiently. This had been the first meaningful conversation that she and I had attempted since the day she packed a bag and walked out the door.

"What do you want me to do about it?" And there it was. I should never have called her. It was a mistake to think she would even, could even care anymore. But she was all I had, and the first person I thought of telling. Five years was a long time to be with someone, and just because she grew apart, didn't mean my feelings weren't still there.

"I guess I just needed to tell someone," I said. She started to say something, but I pulled the phone away from my ear and pressed the END button. She didn't call back.

* * *

"Mind if I sit here?" Reno asked over my left shoulder. I pointed to the empty seat beside me, which he slid into. I poured myself a pint from the pitcher and took a hard pull. Reno sat a glass of ice water down that he had been carrying on the table and pulled a plastic yellow lemon out of his jacket pocket. I watched him pop the little green cap and squirt some into his mouth. He smiled at me and nodded.

"Vocal chords," he said. I nodded back, feigning understanding. "I'm down to sing forth," he explained. I nodded once again, unable to attempt a conversation in the cacophony of the crowd.

I had seen Reno at a few other karaoke contests in the past. We had shared tables before and had attempted whatever passed for conversation between bad renditions of the hits from the 70's, 80's, 90's, and today. He was really good; always seeming to place somewhere in the top three, winning a little cash here and there. These competitions always packed the bars on the weekends. The host establishments made a ton of money off of over-priced, watered down drinks, and they had always footed the prize money. It was a good business model, as it really brought in the crowds. Just like tonight.

The host called out another name and a new singer took the stage. Neil Diamond. Classic and trite; the crowd responded in kind. The bank of lights overhead switched from green to blue to red, trying to pulse along with the music, but seemingly always a bit behind. The dull roar of the crowd diminished some, until the chorus, when everyone shouted their parts like robots programmed to do so. I didn't participate and neither did Reno. He simply tapped his fingers on the side of his glass, beads of condensation rolling over his fingers.

I took another swig from my pint and the waitress stopped at the table, pointing at the half-empty pitcher. I shook my head and she disappeared into the folds of bodies that enveloped our table. I watched Reno's face. His eyes focused on the stage, and I thought I could see the stirrings of nervousness emanate from his mannerisms. I had seen him sing before. He had no reason to be nervous.

* * *

The lab tech squirted some gel into her palm and she rolled it back and forth between hands.

"Trying to get it warm," she explained. I nodded and offered a smile. The gown was pulled up and bunched over my belly. I held my manhood in my hand, as per her instructions. She finally smeared the chilly goo over my testicles, apologizing as she did so. I could feel myself want to contract as the blood drained from my member.

"Okay, hold still." She took the ultrasound wand and pressed down on my balls. I stared at the monitor, equal parts fascinated by what I was seeing, and scared to death of what would be found. There was slight discomfort, which by instinct made me want to squirm away.

"There it is," she said. I stared at it, focusing on the electric image before me. A form the size of a lima bean next to the much larger testicle. A picture of my own personal alpha and omega. I swallowed hard, and faced with the image, I began to think the worst.

"What is it?" I asked. She pressed a button on the machine and the image locked on the screen for a second, and then went back to real time.

"I can't answer that," she said. She rolled the wand over me for a few more minutes, taking more screen shots and then handed me a towel to wipe myself off with. Once I was done, she instructed me to get dressed and wait in the room outside. The towel was starched and scratchy and I did the best I could to clean up. I wanted answers. I needed to know. But she never came back.

* * *

The pitcher was almost empty by the time the third singer took the stage. He was friends with most of the people in the bar, judging by the reaction he got when his name was called. Reno shook his head and sucked some water through his straw.

"He won it last month," he explained. "He used to sing with Fountainhead."

I nodded, acting like I was familiar with Fountainhead and their seemingly long history with lead singers. The crowd fell to a low murmur as he belted out his song, something by Radiohead, I think. The notes were spot on, the melody smooth. The singer knew how to work a stage and the crowd responded in kind. Reno grabbed for the little plastic lemon and squeezed another shot into his mouth.

"I really need to win this," he said. I didn't think he was talking to me. I think he was talking to himself. Pumping himself up. Readying himself for the stage, the mic, the crowd. It was like watching a professional fighter shadow box in the dressing room, working his muscles, preparing for punishment. Reno took a few deep breaths as Mr. Fountainhead finished up his song. The crowd erupted into applause and for the first time, I saw Reno smile. It was now or never.

* * *

I stepped into the doctor's office and saw him seated, a folder open before him. He looked up and smiled, waving his hand toward the empty chair in front of his desk.

"The ultrasound has picked up something," he said as I sat down. "In most instances, it's a simple cyst and isn't cancerous at all. Sometimes it could be epididymitis, which is an inflammation of the epididymis. That's the part of the body where sperm matures before ejaculation."

I tried to follow along. His explanation was long winded, peppered with words I didn't understand. I sat and listened, my mind wandering to what ifs and worst cases.

He flipped the file closed and sat it to the side. A pregnant silence formed between us.

"So, what now?" I asked. He looked at me and I saw the answer clearly all over his face.

* * *

The crowd responded well when Reno's name was called. He slid off his stool and snuck one last sip of his ice water. He fielded a few high fives from the throng behind us as he made his way to the stage. The host handed him the mic and the lights dimmed to a soft blue. The music started and Reno closed his eyes. He brought the mic to his lips and began to sing. The crowd fell into respectful silence. It was a song by U2, soulful and haunting. Reno's voice flowed through the speakers and I watched, afraid to move, afraid to break the melancholic energy that had come over everyone packed into the bar.

As he went into the first chorus, images flashed before my eyes. Pictures of she and I making love in the rain, in the backyard of her parents house during a long Easter weekend. I saw the first apartment we rented as a couple, which was tiny but affordable. I relived the arguments and the fights over the stupidest things, each one stinging due to the perfect vision of hindsight, and the ridiculousness of them all. I saw her, angry and abdicated, as she walked out the door, bag in hand, eyes puffy and red.

We're one, but we're not the same, Reno sang. We got to carry each other, carry each other.

I saw images of the exam, and the technician with cold hands. I saw the doctor, and revisited everything he told me, even that which I didn't understand. And lastly, I saw the form in my hand. An appointment card. For surgery. Set for tomorrow. I finished my pint, in clear disregard to the instructions listed on the surgery prep list. As far as I was concerned, this was my last night on earth. I wouldn't go down without a fight.

Reno finished up the song with two long, pitch-perfect wails. It sent chills down my arms and it brought me back into the present. The last note faded and the people all around me erupted. Reno handed the mic back to the host and pushed his way back to our table. He was assaulted with claps on the backs and half-handed handshakes. He took his seat next to me and sucked a drink through his straw.

"That was amazing," I said.

"Thanks, man," he said. "And thanks for coming out to support me. I couldn't do this shit alone."

I nodded, and raised my empty glass. Nobody should ever have to do this shit alone.

Ghost Runner

Jon Hueber

Brennan recognized the sound. Lacquered wood on leather, tightly rolled twine and cork. Lying on his bed, absently thumbing through a beat-up copy of The Mighty Thor comic book, Brennan looked up and stared out the dirty window, out to the field behind his house where a group of boys were hitting a baseball around. He watched them take turns batting and fielding. They were boys from the other side of the park. Two blocks away, a different world entirely.

Brennan drew away from the window and slid off his unmade bed and kicked a path through the dirty clothes and toys strewn across the bedroom floor. He was a heavy boy, with more than a few pounds of extra weight on his gut and thighs. His face was filled out with jowls that swallowed his cheek bones and chin and made his head as round as a basketball. His sandy blond hair was generally unkempt and dirty, cut by his mother, a novice, using all-purpose shears once a month while Brennan sat on a high back chair in the kitchen. Easily, he was the heaviest of all his friends, and they often let him know it. But that was the life of an eleven year old.

He opened the closet door and dropped to his knees, digging through boxes full of broken GI Joes and armless He-Mans, through shipping cartons full of books and old magazines. He pushed through the tailing ends of hanging collared shirts and church pants until he finally found what he was looking for: His brother's old mitt.

Brennan took the leather glove and slid his pudgy hand into it, working his fingers through the stiff holes. Loose straps of leather hung off, the stitches coming undone with wear and time. The mitt was littered with dark spots, oil that had been over-applied and never wiped off. The glove smelled of must and pine tar and bubble gum and summer. It reminded him of warm nights under fake lights watching his brother play organized Little League ball in the park.

He pulled the mitt off, tied on a pair of Keds, and left the room, glove tucked under his arm. He walked down the creaky wooden staircase, smacking the mitt against the railing in cadence with his steps. In the living room the television was blaring. His mother was watching her stories. The house smelled like boiled chicken and cabbage, though neither was currently on the stove. He walked through the kitchen, his Keds chirping on the tile of the green and white checkered floor and headed toward the door. The screen, ripped in several places, was patched together with a needle and fishing line. The wooden frame was flimsy and warped around the edges, allowing flies to come and go, attracted by the scent of phantom chicken.

Brennan pushed through the door and the spring loudly snapped it shut behind him. He jumped off the top of the stoop onto the dirt floor below. The steps had crumbled the year before and been reset in the spring using concrete and wood. The top step was much higher than the others, a victim of poor planning and worse execution.

Off in the distance, toward the field, he heard laughter and the playful sound of shouting. Brennan walked through the backyard, past the rusted swing set, the slide broken and listing off its anchor to the right. The bolts that kept the frame together were brown with rust, its cancer spreading from the connection points, eating away at the faded green and yellow swirl design that covered the A-frame pipes. Only one swing was still attached, though with his size, he didn't trust the rusty chain that kept the plastic seat suspended from the iron pipe above. Past the swing set was an old Ford LTD sedan, left to die near the back of the lot. The windows were covered in bird droppings and tree sap and dirt. The gold metallic paint was chipped and faded in random spots, long bits of metal framing hanging off the windows like fingers pointing in obscure directions. The rear tires were both flat, long blades of grass growing up and around, claiming the useless rubber wheels as part of their world. Brennan couldn't remember the last time the car had been on the road.

He walked through an opening in the white fence, the gate long since torn off and discarded. The simple, heavily-peeling wooden fence partitioned the backyard from the world beyond. Outside the fence, Brennan crossed the gravel alley, kicking up loose rocks under his heavy footfalls. The field was framed on the western edge by a tall tree line that led into a deep wooded ravine that ended in a winding, and well-travelled parkway that cut through the woods, separating the neighborhood in two; park on one side, houses on the other. In the distance south was an old Masonic Lodge. The lodge owned the land and once a month a fat man on a tractor would spend half a day mowing the grass. The neighborhood had long claimed the land for its own purposes; imminent domain for the children and vagabonds and the occasional rabbit or squirrel.

The lodge itself was a simple white, two-story building, surrounded by large pines that kept the privacy. Brennan had actually never seen any cars parked in the paved lot beside the lodge, and had only seen signs of life there during the annual fish fry held each June. The eastside of the field was separated from the gravel alley by long, tar covered logs, laid end to end. They were retired, well-manicured logs once used as street poles. Some still bore the brass plates and aluminum numbers claiming them for the phone and power companies respectively. Long, rusty nails that once held signs proclaiming yard sales and open houses and lost dogs had been hammered down into the wood, but they could still catch a shoelace or pants cuff if a person wasn't careful. Grass and milkweed grew up around each log, enveloping the dark wood in sun-baked green. The mowers never came close to the logs and nature slowly fought to take the wood back.

Brennan stood there, on the edge of the lot, and saw the group of boys he'd been watching through his bedroom window. There were six of them, all older than he had originally guessed. As he stepped over the line of logs and onto the field itself, he looked at each boy for a flicker of recognition.

The boys were playing a simple game of ball, three on three, two fielders and a pitcher pitching to a group of three batters. The older boys had constructed a makeshift diamond using pieces of cardboard, dirty towels, and salvaged trash. Home plate was a ball glove most likely on loan by the batting team. Brennan slid his brother's mitt on and walked toward the game. The fielders took notice of him, but kept their attention on the game. The pitcher threw an overhand strike that the batter planted through the defense. With two men on, the pitcher took off his red ball cap to wipe the sweat off his brow with the back of his forearm.

"Can I play?" Brennan asked. The boys playing wide second and mid short snickered. The pitcher shot them a glance off his back shoulder that Brennan couldn't see. When he turned back to Brennan, his face was stretched with a smile. Brennan guessed they were all mocking him. He was fat and used to it.

"Sorry, man," the pitcher said. "We got even teams." The last batter stepped into the box and called for a pitch. Brennan stood off to the side, mitt hanging down to his meaty thigh, watching. The sun hung overhead giving off plenty of light and too much heat. Dark circles of sweat were forming under Brennan's arms and he wished he had brought a hat to shield his eyes.

The batter was wearing a Pirates cap, yellow P against black, ending in white plastic mesh that was dirty with age and wear. He swung at an outside pitch and missed. The ball dribbled off and the batter had to scramble out of the box to get it. He tossed the ball back with his left hand and it dropped a few feet in front of the pitcher and rolled. One of the outfielders called him a girl. The batter shouted back with words that would have sentenced Brennan to the corner of the kitchen for a few hours. The next pitch was right down the pipe and the batter swung hard, driving the ball between the pitcher and the boy playing second. The shortstop picked up the ball and threw a bullet back to the pitcher. The bases were loaded.

"Ghost runner," third base called out as he started toward home.

"Wait," the pitcher said. "Why don't we get the fat kid to run for ya?" Brennan's head bobbed with short nods, his eyes open wide accepting the offer before it was even made.

The runner on third base said, "Okay, sure" and Brennan wasted no time getting to the base, an old broken down box of Little Debbie snack cakes. He tossed his brother's mitt off to the side and leaned his body forward, spreading his legs as far as they'd go, right foot pointing toward home, left plated firmly on flimsy cardboard.

"One out," the pitcher yelled. The fielders pounded their fists into their mitts, ready for anything that might come their way.

"You better be ready to hustle there, Porky" the shortstop said. He was taller than the other boys, wearing cut off denim shorts and green-striped tube socks that came up to his knees. His white T-shirt was stained with sweat and he smelled like sour milk and dirty feet, even from a distance. Brennan kept his focus on home and ignored him and his smell.

The batter wore a black KISS T-shirt, the sleeves cut off, the artwork faded. He stepped into the box and took a few practice swings with the bat. Brennan watched him closely, his heart thudding in his chest. He watched the batter and reminisced back to times past watching his brother play for a real team in a real league on a real diamond. The sun above was replaced by tall light poles, blocks of eight, four bulbs over four bulbs. One fixture always seemed to be dimmer than the rest. Swarms of summer bugs danced in front of their illumination, attracted by the light and wary of the bats that would fly by and snatch them out of the air. The grassy field and homemade bases and patchwork t-shirts and hats were replaced by manicured dirt with real chalk lines and rubber bases and matching uniforms with advertisements screen printed on the backs. Brennan could almost smell the boiled hotdogs and nacho cheese and popcorn. He was no longer jealously sitting in the stands watching his brother play. He was on the field. He was in the game. He was the one playing.

The batter connected on the first pitch and the crack of contact snapped Brennan out of his daydream. He saw the batter shoot out of the box, over the glove designated as home plate.

And Brennan ran.

His feet pounded into the ground as hard and as fast as he could muster. His hands balled into tight fists, knuckles white through fat. He kept his elbows in, bracing the girth of his belly from flopping and jiggling as he ran, fists pumping hard. He ran faster than he ever had before. So fast he actually felt the warm breeze of the summer day on his sweaty cheeks and forehead. As he approached home plate he pictured a catcher blocking the bag, readying himself for violent impact. He imagined an umpire, mask in hand, watching the play in the field and turning to officiate the play at home. Imaginary screams erupted from the imaginary stands. Brennan sprung forward, his left Ked landing square on the mitt, his ankle turning a bit. The imaginary umpire shouted him safe and then faded out of existence. The lights were gone. The stands teeming with fans were gone. He was back on the field behind his house, and he was safe.

He turned back toward the field of play, ready for recognition from the older kids for his hustle. Instead, he saw five of the boys standing over the shortstop, who lay motionless on the ground.

Brennan stepped over home plate and walked toward the boys. As he got closer, the shortstop rolled over, away from Brennan's view. Before he could ask what had happened, the shortstop sat up, hands clutching his mouth. Brennan saw red strips of blood rolling through the shortstops fingers and down his hands and wrists, wet and sticky in the sunlight. The older boy was crying.

"I'm so sorry, man," KISS T-shirt said. The other boys looked at him sympathetically. "It was a line drive. I couldn't control it." The shortstop pulled his hand away and spat out parts of teeth, shattered and white in the mix of blood, saliva and snot. His upper lip was split in two and his front teeth, uppers and lowers, were all gone. His bottom lip was already swelling to the size of a small sausage. The blood was pouring out of his face and dribbling off his chin further staining his white T-shirt. The pitcher picked up the towel that was being used as second base, shook out the dirt and grass, and handed it to him.

Brennan stood back, silently watching the older boys rally around one of their own. No one had noticed his hustle. No one had noticed him score. The shortstop cried out again. And Brennan felt like a ghost.

"We better get home," Pirate hat said. "Mom's gonna shit herself." Brennan looked down at the shortstop and back to Pirate hat and saw a familial resemblance, minus the gory mess from the boy on the ground.

"That's game," the pitcher said. "I guessed it's tied."

"I scored," Brennan offered quietly from behind. "Does that count?"

"Yeah," KISS t-shirt said excitedly. "The fat kid scored, we won!"

The shortstop tried to protest, but only succeeded in blowing messy bubbles of blood and goo out of his mouth. The pitcher reached down to help him to his feet. Brennan watched as the other boys collected the mitts and bases. The pitcher and the shortstop were already walking away. The shortstop was stumbling as if drunk.

"Good game," KISS T-shirt said to Brennan. He jogged over to third, picked up Brennan's hand-me-down mitt and threw it to him as hard as he could. Brennan tried to catch it, but clumsily missed and the gloved smacked into his thick chest with a loud thud. Brennan gasped and some of the boys laughed.

"Sorry, man" KISS t-shirt said. Brennan bent over and picked up his brothers glove. His chest stung. He tucked the mitt under his arm and turned away from the remaining boys. He walked slowly back toward his house, stopping once to look back at the group as they walked away, west toward the park. He watched the older boys for a moment or two and thought back to the feeling of actually playing in a game. For a short while, a fleeting moment, he had felt great joy. Forgotten were the beat up comic book he had read more times than he could remember, the cluttered mess that was his bedroom floor (and in many ways, a metaphor of his insipid day-to-day existence), that permanent, gut-wrenching smell of boiled chicken and cabbage, and the back stairs that were crumbled and misshapen which fed into a backyard full of rusted dangers and a useless wreck of a car that would never see the open road again. For an afternoon, Brennan had transcended the doldrums of his own life, and in a moment of clarity, decided he wasn't ready to go back just yet.

Brennan sighed heavily, his face red and dripping with sweat, and pulled the mitt out from under his arm. He slid it over his pudgy hand and squeezed it a few times, breaking in the leather. He walked past his house and made toward the park. He hoped he could find another game with another group of kids, or he could walk down by the creek and catch some crawdads, or whatever else he could find to occupy the rest of this summer afternoon.

A Boy and his Airplane

Teal Schlueter

A boy built an airplane. Huge, with wings large as a house.

Where will the plane sleep? said Father.

At the end of my bed, said the boy. Covered with Grandma's quilt.

Mother was angry because the airplane would piddle on the white carpet.

This must not happen! she said. I will swat the plane with my brush until it learns to go outside or in the sandbox.

Sister said, Yes, I will dress up the airplane in a polka-dotted dress and makeup. Then we shall drink tea.

And the airplane sneaked out the open gate, and later was spotted over West Virginia

by a tobacco farmer.

The Delusional Mister Necessary

Josh Green

Some blond guy is using the Double-Pulley Pulldown when it's my turn. He must be a new member at the gym, because I've never seen his hair before. It seems greatly shampooed, perfect to the point of insult. If my name wasn't Bob Necessary I'd walk up to this guy and ask him where he parked his Pegasus. But my name is certainly that. It has power, even in silence, which means I don't have to confront Hercules, and I won't be talking that Pegasus gibe.

It's right about 8:20 now in the p.m. and primetime for the Spandex rush. It occurs to me nightly that Spandex is a gift from Jesus sent down to middle-aged Midwestern males, a species that includes me. The ladies all look so gifted in Spandex, so properly buttressed. The joy of Spandex holds me over through these winter months until I get the swimsuits I adore at Memorial Public Pool. The red-suited lifeguards in particular. In one-pieces they swim on pool breaks like seals. Their hair, usually blond, is milky in the water, their bodies like limber traces of a dream. Then they pop up for air and chirp about college next year. Hot money I love July.

Spandex on me would be too boastful. On any other man downright flagrant. I prefer gray sweatsuits with high-powered elastic at the ankles. So tastefully accentuating, so perfect for jumping-jacks. Nothing says watch-me-perspire like the wetted Rorschach blots that seep out the back of gray sweats. The attire makes its own remarks so that I seldom have to. Bob Necessary doesn't say what's on his mind. He lets the sweat speak for itself. And tonight I'm on a roll.

Hercules is wrapping up. He tufts back his locks and takes a slow cool gander at the Elliptical girls. He is sniffing my turf. In my younger days, this guy might've been in for a grapple. Or I might've just kicked him in the plums. But now I take the suave approach, the high ground traveled by us more established and gentlemanly beefcakes. I let Hercules wonder and want and then drown in his own soppy bashfulness. He's too shy to make the approach. Like the rest of us, I bet he's hatched a thousand hypotheses about courting gym women but has acted on none. Nobody talks in these places. They just peek. They keep eyes on the fanning deltoids of the ship-shape crowd around them but never mouth a word.

There goes Hercules. Turning around, retreating from the Ellipticals, not a chance. He shows his back to the cardio crew and hawks another machine, defeat at its puniest. Finally he sits on the Lower Back Extender and rows his invisible boat, his sorry tattoos peeking out from the unwashed white T.

I take his place triumphantly. In a burst of sheer explosive might I latch onto the Pulldown and enjoy the view: every floppy breast Flecksers Fitness has to offer. The mirrored walls, the hanging plasmas, the rows of joggers, the Spandex princesses on big pink Ab Balls, the meatheads slapping chalk. It's the busiest hour. For twenty-two dollars per month and no contractual obligations this place is mine. In the mirror now, beyond the Incline Bench and the Calf Raiser, my head looks fantastic. Not bald but with wings of hair. I pull down—herrrmph! And let back up—fffsssooo! I conquer the Pulldown and everybody takes notice.

A brunette is headed this way, one o' clock. She looks so familiar, and so stern. The insignia on her shirt is authoritative and brassy. It shines under the gym's heavy halogen. She's so close I can read her nametag—Monica. She has forearm veins.

"Mr. Necessary?" says Monica. "Can you hear me? Please take off the Walkman."

"Yes?" I slip off the headset, so padded with orange foam. The sound of early Men At Work fades onto my shoulders, cascades down my chest. "Bob, please. Hello."

"Alright, Bob. Did you check in when you came through? At the front desk?"

"Yes," I say. "Certainly."

"Funny," says Monica. "You're not electronically registered as being in here. And technically you're not allowed back in Flecksers in the first place. Our records still show you haven't paid in three months. We can't auto-draft from your checking because you have no available funding."

"Can you say that more quietly around here?" I put a finger on my lips. "We have reputations to uphold."

Monica huffs, hands on her hips. She isn't treading lightly. She's pumped. Must be the creatine kicking in.

"I have committed no incidents of misbehavior here," I say. "As I told you last month, your payments are en route. Have some patience, I'm a very busy man."

"Mr. Necessary, I'm sorry. This is a business and I manage it at night. It's important to wean your muscles slowly, so I'll let you finish your routine this evening. Go light weight and high reps. After that, you can't come back in here."

"Not even for jumping-jacks?"

"No, the gym is for paying members only. You can't come in the door."

"Answer me one question," I say.

"If you come back in," says Monica, getting fussy, "I'll have to call the Westport Police. You'll technically be trespassing."

"One question?"

"One question."

I stand up and turn halfway around. "My posterior," I say. "How's it coming?"

She takes an admiring glance.

"Lumpy," she says. "Like mashed potatoes."

I feel a burn but not the burn. This Monica must be writhing with passion—I can see it in her mandibles. But I can't think of anything to say in return, so I pull my Walkman back on. She juts up her left fingers and circles the right ones for numerical significance: four and zero, I guess. Then she says, loudly, over the didgeridoo in my mind, "Forty minutes, Mr. Necessary. That's it. We close in forty."

Truth be told, I wasn't always so Necessary. I was on the football team at Chesapeake High School but otherwise this (specimen that is me) could not have been predicted. Mother had seen it coming but nobody else did. With her red cheeks like gelatin she told me late-bloomers do bloom best. That was a very long time ago, 1981, and bloom I did: two hundred fifty pounds now of prime man-beef, a chunk of rippling granite, a walking anatomy lesson. Mother was right on the money.

In my football years I played the offensive line. I brought glamour to the trenches. With me on the field the underclass girls were prone to swooning. That didn't sit well with the rock-brained football lords. I was whipped by towels so hard one time they broke open my back and ass cheeks. I can still see the blood whirlpooling in the locker-room shower drain. That happened late in the football season, so late I couldn't wear jeans or wool sweaters for a family Thanksgiving photo at Willard's Department Store. The last photo before dad choked to death and I couldn't even sit down.

Dad was a winner. And smart beyond his janitorial duties. He told me one time our family name had been translated from the opening stanza of a Norwegian battle cry. He was romantic like that, as most habitual liars are. But his lies were benign and funny, so far beyond the truth they landed feather-soft. The only collateral damage was the hollowness it created in him. He got to the point he couldn't believe himself, and when that happens it's best to keep on lying. In fact I thought he was joking when he turned purple and clutched his throat during Ten Cent Oyster Night at the Wok N' Roll Buffett. It was Thursday, our weekly father-son dinner after football practice, and I just sat there, laughing uproariously, until a waiter got wise and screamed for a doctor.

"What's your problem?" the waiter hissed. "That dumb look on your face at a time like this. Do something!"

When they pronounced dad expired and crated him away I finished my plate. Call me sordid but it's the truth. I sucked every husk of edamame empty, devoured each shred of ginger, and scarfed the whole stack of moo shoo pancakes. I ate until my belly popped over my football tights. Eating that much felt like a blanket on my insides. It would be my new defense—caloric impalement.

In order to uphold my sexiness, I needed plenty of sweating, and for continued sanity I required loads of thinking time. The rank fumes of old gymnasiums called to me like sirens' songs. In gyms I was nobody's fool, a coward no longer, anybody I could imagine. Public exercise lent me a new perspective on the world and all its flawed inhabitants at their most primal. I joined the Westport YMCA and worked my way up.

A man in my position loves a challenge. Monica has no idea. Bob Necessary fills his lungs with the odor of challenge and expels the fabulous fumes of victory. In forty minutes I can attract flocks of Spandex. But I've never responded well to deadlines. Mother allowed me years to triumph.

Before Monica can strut back to the front desk (where she'll peck through Physical Science 301 material instead of working, as always) I spot several Necessary candidates treading away like hamsters beneath the plasmas. They're watching a brainless game show. They laugh at the blinking numbers and they are transfixed. I disqualify them immediately. Not worthy.

On the Exerbike is what looks to be a deranged Irish midwife. She sifts through underwear ads in a colorful magazine filled with celebrity schlock. She has a hideous pucker-face but a fine, fine posterior. It teeters like a sideways eight on the bike seat, half-expanding and half-contracting with the movement of her hindquarter pleasantries. Next to her is a massive brother drenched in tribal tattoos. They could be together, the housewife and the brother, which isn't worth the chance. It's unsettling to know what'll happen to such a tall man when I make him fall. Plus it could strain my hamies to kick so high.

I'm feeling a change of scenery. I walk across the red carpet to the rubberized floor area, nearly undoing the Velcro on my sneakers. Here I find the Cable Sitdown Bench, which I know comes with many great angles. From here I can see the Dip Assist, the Squat Rack, the Lateral Flex and, should I catch the right combination of mirrored images, up to the panties of a loose-shorted lady on the Decline Bench.

Here, the Spandex glows in the gymnasium's far corners. It takes a while to find it all. I have to peer back and forth through the mirror until the really brilliant stuff pops out, like Easter eggs in the grass.

Nothing is popping tonight, however. No eggs, no grass. Only sweatpants and loose button-ups and too-thick clothing. A gray blur jostles at low speed on the equipment around me. There are very old women here, some with very old men. These pairings only amplify the lurking nervousness behind my abs, so I have to look away.

The tape clicks to an end and the music in my ears stops. Outside, streetlights flicker on a steely yellow streetscape. A wet dog, a German shepherd perhaps, chases a tumbling Burger Buddy wrapper down a dark alley. The dog disappears into shadow and my feeling is that it will never catch up.

And then He enters.

The gym patrons fall silent, the glass doors open. A gust of wind announces the entrance of the man I've named Brutor in my mind, the absolute alpha meathead. He is incredible, this Brutor, all six feet nine of Him, the hulking trunk of Him. He rips off His trench coat and shoves the bundle of it in a locker. Even Monica stares. On His big feet are white and red high-tops, untied. Across the wide waves of His chest is always a T-shirt, usually red, brandishing the old Music Television logo. Tonight He's dressed as usual, like a Russian pitfighter in basketball gear.

Brutor walks in huge impressive steps, and without exception He walks toward me. Everything that comprises Him is superior to the composition of me. Among this Flecksers tribe He has no rival, only silent admirers. Other patrons sigh.

"Is this bench free, jumping-jack?" Brutor says.

I pretend to not hear because looking up to Brutor makes me feel so small.

"You on here or not?" he asks, to which I do not reply. I sense mirrored eyeballs on us. "Then get up and spot me," he says. "Do you want me to get pissed?"

I stand up for Him but I step backwards, nearly tripping on a Triceps Rope with fat rubber handles. I have never understood how one man can spot another on a machine with cables, yet He always demands it of me. It makes Him appear even bigger with me nearby, and I don't want that comparison to ruin my last night. He hovers over me, pokes my back, quips about my sweatpants, and there is nothing I can do. I want to call Brutor a chest-pounding, veined-out megalomaniac with nothing better to do at 8:50 in the p.m. on a Wednesday night. But I wouldn't do that. I don't need to say that. Then again I need to say something at some point. It's just that my bones don't feel secure enough within me to say anything at all.

Brutor rips into the exercise and I dissipate into the squirm. In His every heave and grunt I see an awesomeness that can never be mine. His routine is gaining fury and He hasn't noticed my leaving. He is the only one allowed to keep pumping after close. Rumor has it He stays and rips away in the dark.

In my one year at Elizabeth State College, the kids in my dorm dubbed me "Megadork," and "Dorkosaurus," and "Dorky Dorkerton." It was too much to handle, being cooped in classrooms with jealous nincompoops of that caliber. One night in my room, they pushed a drunk girl in and held the door closed behind her. She had money in her hand and red lipstick on so thick it was nearly dripping. She bent over my comic and crammed her tongue in my mouth. I had drunk a lot of Muscle Milk before bed and so I peed myself. She screamed, pulled a tiny camera from her pocket, and immortalized me with a flash-bulb picture, the wetness like an aerial shot of Africa.

I dropped out and never officially got certified in applied electronics.

Mother didn't care. She wanted me around as much as possible. It didn't feel right being away from her anyhow. By leaving the dorm I could snuggle with Mother during the evening news and bake the snickerdoodles she can't live without.

We continue the news-and-cookies ritual to this day. She's becoming somewhat brittle, so I have to mind the placement of my hands, strong as they are. I can tell it's her favorite time, our evenings together, just her and me and the anchormen with great hair. There, on the couch with her only child, my Mother kind of blossoms. She even talks sometimes between gulps of sorbet and cookie dough. Like me, Mother clammed up after dad's sudden passing. The way I see it, that doesn't mar her qualities. She embodies every single thing I could desire in a woman, with the exception of fitness, personality, and intelligence.

Sometimes at night I take a flashlight under the covers and explore old family photo albums. I can tell that, as a baby, I was a blessing to Mother and dad. Those sepia photos with curved corners tell me so. I flip the pages and voyage to places I've been but don't recall. The vacation pictures stick with me the most. I lie awake and imagine myself at Myrtle Beach, building sand forts with dad. I see us pulling balloons together through Battery Park in New York City. I watch him carry me like his own personal Medicine Ball, a dying Miami sunset over our shoulders.

Monica is at the entrance desk with her heels propped on a Formica countertop. Come to think of it, her legs aren't shabby. She chews a thick wad of bubble gum in voracious, churning bites. She flips into her book as if she doesn't know I'm leaving. I approach the exit with eight minutes to spare.

"What should I do with the towel?" I ask, and she looks up, bedazzled. I watch the pupils of her eyes adjust from the tiny print of her reading material to the stunning visage of me. Maybe she's vexed by the question. "The towel. It was issued to me when I became a member. Now I'm not one. Should I take it? I'm very sweaty. Well, usually I am."

"It's yours," says Monica, and she slips back into her reading.

"If I want to come back, do I have to pay for all the months at once?"

"Yep," she says.

A cold silence. She isn't even looking at me. The overhead racket of heavy metal guitars is not what I want to hear. I toss the towel over my shoulder and pull my house key from the clothespin to which I hook it in my pocket. I don't drive here; I walk it. The house where Mother waits is just up the street.

"I run a small business, and times are slow right now," I say. "I also take care of my Mother. For rent mostly, but it's a big job. She went all catatonic after dad died."

"I'm sorry," Monica says. "Cancer?"

"Not even close," I say. "He was setting a world record for the largest oyster ever consumed. We come from a seafaring people. Anyhow, he choked."

"He choked on an oyster?"

"Yes, sadly."

"I thought that was impossible."

"It was the size of a baby's head."

"Huh," she says. "That's tragic."

"As I was saying, Mother needs plenty of looking after. It's good for me to come here during breaks with her."

Monica perks. "So you still live with your mom?"

I have to gather myself a second, wipe my palms across my thighs.

"My skill is to fix video game machines," I say. "I'm good at it. I've practiced for over twenty years. It's just that the kind I fix are the ones nobody plays anymore."

Another silence.

"It's hard to believe you're not married, Mr. Necessary," says Monica. "The ladies in here are missing out on a real prince."

"How'd you know that?"

"You're listed as single in our records."

"You checked?" I ask with considerable pep.

Monica sits up slowly. "I was searching for an alternate source of income in your family," she says, flipping her eyelashes in a final rejection. "You're so full of the wrong ideas."

I slip the silent headphones back over my ears and exit Flecksers Fitness. Harsh, wet winds bite at my hands. I turn around to walk backwards, now halfway across the parking lot, and I expect to see the entire gym clamoring at the windows to know where I'm going. Of course they're not doing that. The silly activities are going on without me. The gymnasium squirms and squirms. Nobody in there is perfect enough, not even Brutor. In and out, up and down, the futile pursuit of absolutely nothing. I wish the windows would suddenly fog over and stay that way.

Hovering in a huge illuminated rectangle above the fitness center is the billboard that first got me to join. It was glowing in the night, like now, with its low monthly figures scribbled in cursive red. On the billboard is a shirtless man with a superbly white smile and huge hands that I could just crawl into. The underline of his pectoral muscles is glorious and cut, the same with his outer delts. I take a seat on a curb in the parking lot and sit half-covered by a bush. Blanketing myself with the gym towel, I pull my knees into my chest, give a little cough, and then I push my right thumb behind my teeth and onto my tongue, biting down. In my suckling I feel the folds of thumb-skin with my curious tongue. The thumbnail itself is smooth. I watch the billboard as its lights flicker. Up there the teeth and hair and manicured nails are really booming. I can see the serendipity between the letters and the skin. And yes the twinkle of eternal galaxies goes on behind the man forever.

They Pressed Quietly

Jessica Dyer

I have found it,
the root
of discomfort:
they slipped between
me and myself
and the flowered
secret given
to all girls.

But it is just
an idea,
an experiment
a touched untouchable,
not formal
or intimate;
too many hands,
considered normal,
pressed
over my
lacking body.

One asks why can't
I feel beautiful
when naked,
and I say
quietly
it's situational.

in small sections

Jessica Dyer

i.
like so many petals
dropped
peeled apart
at the base
lost in the rotting
world of lichen,
the dead sing
we are the dust
and we are the divine

ii.
we are all stuck—
flecks of skin inside
the black sweater
of a whirling monster.

sunday morning and the sun is still rising

Jessica Dyer

it will melt the new frosted
fog on my window, splay
across strands of pearls—
forgotten ships,
droplets on a dark sea of papers,
lost among colding coffee
in antique mugs, coupons
clipped at midnight—
lustrous and storied
and my hardened fingers
knotty from nearing winter

Oak Floors and Drafty Windows

Megan Anderson Hamand

The house was nothing but old-fashioned when Mark and his new bride bought it. The floors were oak, the walls papered, the kitchen cabinets metal, and the windows drafty. Despite of all that, Mark's wife fell in love with it right away. She said it was reminiscent of her grandmother's house with its hardwood floors, wallpapered rooms, single-paned windows, and metal cabinets. Mark had been a sucker for anything his wife wanted—though he thought the house was too drafty and the floors too hard to comfortably lay down on—so he took out a thirty-year mortgage and began working to pay it off. The marriage only lasted ten years, and Mark was stuck with the drafty windows, papered walls, oak floors, and metal cabinets for at least another twenty.

"Your mom is leaving," Mark had told his son, eight-years-old at the time.

"When is she coming back?"

"I'm not sure," Mark answered. "But when she does come back, she probably won't live with us anymore."

"Why not?"

"The windows are too drafty for her. You know how she's cold all the time," Mark said. "She wants to live somewhere that's warmer."

"Why can't we all live somewhere that's warmer?"

"Because you and I like this house too much."

"Oh."

As Landen grew older, he didn't believe Mark's fake answers about why his mom left, but Mark couldn't bring himself to confess the whole truth: she left because she was sick of being a wife and a mother, and she had a new dream—writing a gossip column about celebrity's love lives for a big city newspaper. So she moved to Chicago, but the only job she could get at a newspaper was writing obituaries for the Sun Times when the regular writer was sick or on vacation.

With his wife gone and a twenty-year mortgage on his hands, Mark was left to try to make the 19th century house a home. He put up a wallpaper border with footballs, basketballs, and soccer balls in Landen's room, but it started to fall down after only a year. Landen didn't mind though; he said he was too old for a sports border. Mark bought a big screen TV for him and Landen to bond in front of while watching Die Hard movies and Notre Dame football games, but when they went to rearrange the living room furniture, they realized the dirty green of the wallpaper had faded everywhere but where the TV stood, leaving a dark square of wallpaper on the north wall. Mark forced Landen into a mandatory-fun day of repainting the house siding, but as soon as they finished power sanding the white paint, Landen left to play basketball with his friends. After that Mark gave up trying to get his son interested in the house. He left the border peeling from the wall, the unfaded square of wallpaper in the living room, and the sanded-off paint on the outside of the house.

With his wife gone, Mark made himself concentrate on his job, his son, and his house, though none of these were too rewarding. He worked at a fertilizer plant—bringing the smell home with him every night—fixing trucks and machinery. It was a mindless job that he dreaded going to every morning. He didn't understand his own son, and they barely spoke, except when Landen asked for money. He said lunch money, but Mark had his doubts. And the house was still falling apart around him. Restoring it to its original, old-fashioned design seemed like too much work, so he turned his attention to making it more modern.

Mark spent every night after work for two weeks tearing out the metal cabinets in the kitchen. He wanted to put in new, cherry wood ones, with a revolving corner door for canned vegetables and boxes of macaroni and cheese—all Mark really knew how to make for supper—and a cutting board that pulled out as a drawer, though Mark didn't know how to slice and dice enough to have the use for a cutting board. Two nights of his laboring was spent simply emptying the cabinets and stacking the contents in the dining room—it hadn't been used for meals since Mark and his wife were newlyweds—making piles and piles of pink-flowered china—also hadn't been used since the beginning happy period of his marriage—plastic cups, silverware, and hand-me-down pots and pans from Mark's mom.

Landen waded to him through the mess of china and pans on the second night of emptying the cabinets. Mark was still working, but only had the ones above the stove left, so there seemed like an end in sight.

"I'm going out," Landen said as he stepped over and around plastic cups and coffee mugs to the closet where his pleather, biker jacket hung.

Mark looked up from his work to his watch. Eleven o'clock. "It's way too late for you to just now be going out," he said. "It's Tuesday night."

"So?"

Mark stepped off of the kitchen chair—he was too short to reach the cabinets above the stove without assistance—and tiptoed his way into the dining room around the dishes tipping over in stacks on the floor. "Sooooo, it's too late."

Landen gave him a like-I-care look with raised eyebrows and a smirk playing on the corners of his mouth and continued to put on his jacket and tan work boots. Mark made his way over to the door and put his hands on his hips, trying to look as authoritative as possible, but Landen rolled his eyes, still smirking, and walked past him into the night street.

So Mark finished the kitchen by himself, never asking Landen for help and Landen never offering it. Finishing it meant, of course, that the cabinets were completely torn out but new cabinets were yet to be installed. Mark shopped at Home Depot once but couldn't found anything he liked, or that he thought Landen would like. So Mark told himself he would keep looking and not settle for something that looked remotely old fashioned. He had in mind what he wanted. He knew the cherry red wood-finished cabinets would not match the rest of the kitchen décor—mustard yellow paint on the walls with 1970's style flowers of the same nauseating color as a border going around the top of the kitchen—but he had plans to change the colors after the cabinets were installed.

With the kitchen cabinets done in his mind, Mark started on the wallpaper in the living room. He wanted to rearrange the furniture—including the big screen TV—and paint it a tan color. The color wouldn't match the maroon and dark blue floral couch and loveseat, but the furniture was soon to be modernized as well. So Mark spent an entire Saturday and Sunday ripping down wallpaper.

It was fun and easy at first. He grabbed a loose edge of wallpaper by the ceiling, closed his eyes, picturing the unfaded square of musty green wallpaper, and yanked down with all his anger and might. The first piece came completely off, baring scraps of newspapers and an uneven wall underneath. The newspaper didn't come off as nicely. Mark pulled quickly and painlessly—like he had watched his wife pull bandaids off of Landen's scraped knees when he was little—but along with the newspaper came pieces of the decaying wall, making it more uneven.

Mark was able to get all the wallpaper—but not the newspaper—off of the wall where the TV once stood, and he began to paint it with the caramel tan paint he bought on clearance from the hardware store. As he worked the next Saturday, trying to cover the uneven wall with bits of newspaper still stuck to it, he heard Landen come down the creaking stairs. His eyes were still cloudy from sleeping—it was 1 p.m.—and he was still wearing the Nine Inch Nails t-shirt from the night before.

"Your mom called this morning," Mark told his son.

"That's nice."

"She called collect, again," Mark said as his soaking paint brush dripped paint on the oak edge board that he forgot to tape off. He smeared the paint into the grains of the wood as he tried to scoop it up with his finger.

"Maybe if you'd send her some money she wouldn't have to call collect," Landen said as he walked into the kitchen looking for breakfast or lunch.

"I'm the one with the kid. Shouldn't she send me money?" Mark yelled across the living room and dining room into the kitchen.

"Whatever," Landen muttered.

Mark joined his son in the kitchen and sat on the step stool. "She called to tell you happy birthday." Landen snorted. "I know. She's a little late—"

"Like a month late."

"Yeah, okay, a month late. But at least she called," Mark said.

"Whatever."

Mark only finished painting the wall of the living room that held the TV—it still held the TV because he didn't have the energy to move the furniture around—because the other walls did not give up its wallpaper as easily as the first, though he was glad to have something to tear down after paying an extra fifty cents on his phone bill for the collect call from Chicago. Plus, the painted wall looked like it had been beaten and battered with holes and dents shining through the caramel paint. Mark quickly realized why the entire house had been wallpapered.

So he moved onto the oak floors that continuously squeaked and handed out splinters on his bare feet. Carpeting, he decided he needed carpeting on all of the downstairs floors. He wanted to keep the oak floors on the stairway because the creaking and moaning of the warped wood gave away Landen's location in the middle of the night. Since the two rarely spoke, and a pleasant conversation was even rarer, the steps were sometimes the only indication Mark had of Landen's whereabouts. So Mark picked out carpeting for the living room and family room. The dining room would have to stay uncarpeted since the floor was unreachable because the dishes from the kitchen still claimed the room.

Mark went to the carpet outlet on the east side of town, where he discovered drug dealers owned the street corners—Mark swore he saw Landen standing with them once—and the best deals were to be found on anything from carpeting to cocaine. Mark bought as much dark purple carpeting with light pink droplets that the store had. They offered free installation, but he was trying to modernize the house with his own two hands so he could take some pride in the remodeling, even though professionals would no likely do a better job. After laying the carpet in the family room, though, Mark came to the discovery that although he bought out the store of this particular style of carpeting, he didn't have enough to do the living room wall-to-wall, so he'd have to improvise.

One afternoon, after Mark had gathered up the energy to move all of the living room furniture—the big screen TV included—into the completely carpeted family room, he called Landen out of hiding in his room to help make the decision of where to position the carpeting. At least three feet of one side of the room was going to remain uncovered, and Mark couldn't decide whether it should be the east or west side.

"Either way it's going to look stupid," Landen said, being very helpful in Mark's opinion.

"I know," Mark said shaking his head. He was still in disbelief that the $200 spent on carpeting still wasn't enough. "If you leave the east side uncovered, then you won't notice right away, since you enter on the other side. But, if we leave the west side uncovered, you won't really notice when you're sitting on the couch."

"Either way people are going to notice."

"I know," Mark said through gritted teeth.

"Why didn't you just buy enough carpeting? And why did you pick such an ugly, girly color? It looks retarded. It's not like Mom's going to come back and would like this girly stuff anyway."

Mark looked up from smoothing the carpet. "Where did that come from?"

"What?" Landen shrugged his shoulders.

"Where did that come from?" Mark looked hard at his son, who was tugging on the carpeting, as if to stretch it to fit the whole room. Mark's back cracked in four different places as he struggled to his feet to look his son in the eyes.

"You think by redoing this damn house, fixing the cabinets, laying carpeting, she's going to come back? I doubt she left because she hated the house. She probably left because she hated us. Or just you. Who knows? But you should just stop with the damn home improvements. You're just making everything worse anyways." By the end of his speech, Landen was yelling. He stood up—without any cracks sounding in his back—and glared at Mark before leaving the room.

After leaving the east end of the living room uncarpeted, Mark moved onto fix the windows. He had plans to remove and redo all of the downstairs ones. After a restless night of dreaming about his wife and the adventures she was now having as an obituary writer in Chicago where she didn't make enough money to make a five-minute, long-distance phone call to her son a month after his birthday, he got up in the middle of the night to begin measuring the windows in the family room. As he worked, he heard Landen come down the stairs.

"What the hell are you doing, Dad?" he asked, not sounding at all groggy for it being 2:15 in the morning.

Without even turning around, Mark answered, "Measuring the windows."

Landen collapsed on the loveseat in the family room. "Please, no more home improvements." Mark put the tape measure down and looked at his son. "Mom isn't coming home if you fix up this house. Besides, you're trying to make it more modern, and she liked the old fashionedness of it."

Mark joined Landen on the black leather love seat that he recently bought it at auction from an unfortunate tax dodger. "I'm not fixing the house up to get your mom back." He was silent for a moment. "I'm fixing the house up for you."

"Well, I'm like Mom," Landen said, though Mark knew there was more truth in those words than his son meant. "I like the house when it was all old and crap. I hate all this new shit you've been trying. It looks like . . . shit." Landen stood up. "I'm going back to bed. Could you keep the racket down and not freaking wake me up again?"

Mark nodded, very doubtful that Landen had ever been asleep.

The next morning, Mark—after calling in sick at work, though he hadn't thrown out his back like he told the foreman—dragged the old metal kitchen cabinets out of the garage where he had stored them until he got around to taking them to the junkyard. After a whole day of struggling—and with Landen's volunteered help—Mark reinstalled the cabinets he had hated since the day his wife convinced him to buy the house.

At Landen's suggestion, though, the cabinets were repainted. With a new coat of clean, white paint, they looked more like how they were meant when originally installed in the 1930s.

Also at Landen's urging, Mark moved all the furniture out of the family room and living room—he was able to store it in the dining room now that the dishes were finally put back in the metal cabinets—and tore up the dark purple carpeting. The two rented a power sander, sanded the floors, and—together—started to restain the oak floors.

As Landen stained the family room, Mark worked in the living room. He yelled across the rooms: "Your mom didn't leave because she was too cold."

Mark heard Landen slowly put down his paint brush, stand up, stretch his legs, and walk into the living room. "What?" he asked.

"Your mom didn't leave because the drafty windows made her too cold," Mark repeated. "She moved to Chicago to be a gossip columnist. But she could only get a job as a part-time obituary writer."

Landen shook his head. He didn't seem surprised with this new knowledge of his mother. "I knew she didn't leave because of the house, Dad," he said. He picked up another paint brush and dipped it into the stain to help finish the living room floor. "Look at this house," he said with a smile. "It's gorgeous, so I always knew that wasn't why."

Mark smiled and continued working.

After another moment of silence, Landen said, "Next can we work on that terrible sports border you insisted on putting up in my room?"

Storm Chasers

Russell Puntenney

We go down by the river every time it rains,
Lose all sense of direction in the spattering mess.
The raindrops whisk up, the river flows down,
And we float, caught in bliss,
Caught somewhere in the middle
Of bedrock and cloud.

Just me and the water and sweet Angeline,
Just me and the sky and the shambles below.
We see minnows and crawdads and mist in the air,
We hear thundering crashes and two beating hearts.
There's a tree losing leaves,
There's an angel shining bright,
And sometimes it seems
There's just me.

When the storm clouds disperse, we dry off and depart,
Naming the birds as they sing back to life.
There's nothing to fear once that thunder subsides,
Nothing to fear now that all is reborn.
Up's up again,
Down's back to down,
Nothing to fear,
Not anymore,
While to some,
There never really was.

Our Bench in the Park

Ronald Short

I sat there in the middle of that park, a cold bench beneath me and my breath burning my lungs as I tried to catch it in the brisk December air. I sat there just waiting. Waiting for that moment to come and be over with. My hands were moist with nervousness under my wool gloves. I didn't know what to expect. At this point I believed anything could happen.

She approached me with haste. She was tall and slender like a runway model. The parts of her long brown hair not held down by her stocking cap blew in the icy wind as she approached me in slow motion. Everything had moved to slow motion, like all of those cheesy 80s movie sequences where the love interest enters into the protagonist's life. It quickly became my favorite memory of all. As she got closer, I saw how full her lips were and how red and cracked they had become because of this harsh New York winter. Mother Nature could do her worst and even then she wouldn't ruin this thing of beauty.

Her cheeks were kissed with the slightest of freckles and her big green eyes sparkled with the reflection of the snow. This was the most beautiful woman I had ever seen. I would have waited days on this bench for her. She jogged up with a look of worry as she sat down beside me and placed her hand upon my leg.

"What took you so long?" I asked.

She responded with a, "What?"

"I've been waiting so long for you and you finally decide to show up now?"

"I . . . I'm sorry."

You could tell she was truly sorry and I didn't want to press the issue any further.

"I'm just glad you came," I said. "It wouldn't have been fun to be stood up in the cold."

She forces a smile. I can't tell if it's because she's awkward in these types of situations or if she just isn't as attracted to me as I am to her. I push forward.

"What's your name?" I asked.

"Lynn."

"What a simple name for a complex beauty such as yourself."

There it was. The genuine smile I had been waiting for. She wiped what I believe was snow from her face with her mittens as a slight laugh escaped her mouth. A hard cough hit me, which quickly erased the smile from her face.

"Excuse me," I said as I wiped my mouth with the handkerchief I kept in my pocket.

"I told you mine," Lynn said. "It's only fair that you tell me yours."

"Joe," I muttered as I cleared my throat of the remains of that last cough.

"You look like a Joe."

"Do I? What does a Joe look like, if you don't mind me asking?"

"I dunno. Rugged, handsome, has a certain swagger about them."

"You think I'm handsome, aye?" I asked as I forced my own smile in the cold wind.

She looked at me through her green thirty-something year old eyes with an honesty I had never seen in any woman's eyes before. Why did she have to come at this moment? Why couldn't she have come sooner, saved me from past mistakes? I've been on this earth forty eight years. Have had relationships with several women in that time and none of 'em looked at me like that. The mother of my child never even looked at me like that.

"I think it's cruel what fate does to us, ya know?"

"What is it that fate does to us?" asked Lynn as she wiped more snow from her face.

"I've been looking for someone like you my whole life. Someone who makes a snowy day such as this seem like the sunniest and brightest day I've ever been a part of. Someone who could make a cancer patient feel cured after a smile. Someone who makes me feel like the most important person in the world by just the way they look at me. Fate decides to place you in my life now when I could have been spending my whole existence with you."

"Joe . . . you barely know me. We've only just met."

"By all means; tell me everything. I want to know all about you."

Lynn is reluctant at first. I know this was merely our first meeting, but I wanted to make up for lost time. I prayed that she will release the floodgates and will tell me her life story.

"I . . . uh . . . I love the Giants. They are my favorite football team," she said.

"So far, off to a good start," I responded.

"My favorite movie is The Godfather."

"Oh, come on," I teased. "If you're going to like any movie in the crime genre it has to be Goodfellas. It's hands down the best."

"Maybe in your opinion, man, but The Godfather's where it's at for me," she teased back with a big smile on her face.

"All right, to each their own. You are one for two right now," I quipped with a smirk.

"My favorite food is Chicago style pizza."

"You're a brave one to admit that here in the Apple."

We both shared a smile and then I noticed her gaze. It's one of those gazes that you catch in passing as someone is falling in love with you. At least, that's what I had hoped it was. She quickly shook it off, wiped more snow from her face, and continued as if it hadn't happened. The wind was drying out my eyes so I decided to close them. Lynn shook me hard and my eyes jerked back open.

"You haven't told me about yourself," she said with concern.

"I'm far less interesting, I can assure you."

"Please," she insisted with glossy eyes. The wind must have gotten to her, too.

"I . . . uh, am also a Giants fan. My favorite movie is Goodfellas and I, too, love Chicago style pizza."

"Traitor," she teased.

"I'm also a man who has made a lot of mistakes," I confessed as if she was a priest and I was in a confessional. It all just seemed to pour out. "I own my own business over in the Bronx. A little coffee shop. I don't know what I was thinking going against Starbucks and then this economy. It hasn't been the best of times."

I paused for a moment and took a deep breath.

"Please, continue," she urged. "You can tell me anything you want."

"I'm telling you, a lot of mistakes," I continued. "I have a son from my marriage to my wife Carrie. We're divorced now, but I've made sure to be a part of my son's life. He just got into college recently, a real prestigious school, ya know? He got a lot of scholarships and grants, but it's one of those schools where those things just won't cover it all. I wanted to help him out the best I could, so I went to this guy I knew through my friend Bill . . ."

A strong cough interrupted my train of thought. This time, it was a barrage of hacking that wouldn't stop for a good thirty seconds. I covered my mouth as blood started to spray onto my glove. The coughing stopped as I tried to calm my heart.

"I apologize for sharing so much on our first date," I said through pained voice. "It's just so easy to open up to you."

"It's fine . . . just fine," she said quivering.

It was at that moment I noticed how red her eyes had become. She wiped her face again, but it wasn't snow she was wiping away. I finally realized it had never been snow. It was tears.

As I tried to move my hand closer to her face to comfort her, a sharp pain stopped me in my tracks. The bullet in my gut had moved further in and the blood began to flood out of the gaping wound into the puddle in the snow.

"Sir, stay still," said a voice from behind Lynn. "Help is on the way."

I opened my eyes wide to see a crowd of people surrounding us that I didn't notice or didn't want to notice before. They all watched as Lynn comforted a dying sad sack on a park bench. My eyes grew heavier.

"Lynn . . . could you tell me something?" I asked.

"Yes, of course."

"Do you think you would have gone for a guy like me? You know, in different circumstances?"

"Yes, I think I would."

"Lynn . . . I'm sorry if this is too soon, but . . . I love you. With all my heart. I love you."

"I love you, too, Joe."

I heard sirens in the distance and Lynn's heavy weeping as my eyes closed shut.

Joe sat at that park bench in the middle of Central Park as he does every Monday morning. He sipped on his freshly brewed coffee and read his New York Times as he watched the morning passerby's go along through their day. Seeing people merely living their lives brought joy to Joe, especially as he got older and began thinking about his own mortality. In about an hour, Joe would be opening shop for what might be the last day of business. People just didn't see the appeal of his shop, he thought. He would never be able to pay off his debts if he kept it open. Tomorrow, he'd be signing the papers to sell it to another proprietor.

It was a solemn day for Joe. He had been working to get this shop since he was twenty years old and was finally able to secure it five years ago. He somehow kept it alive up to this day, but he could do it no longer. His son needed to go to college and he had a debt to pay off.

As Joe took another long sip on his coffee, made from his own recipe, a man with a pea coat pulled tight around his body sat next to him. The man had a grizzly beard, a scar across his right cheek, and a black beanie on top of his head with a button displaying a skull pinned onto the front.

"Can't a man enjoy his coffee in peace?" asked Joe.

"We need that money, Joe," said the man.

"I am signing my building over to a guy tomorrow morning," responded Joe. "I will have the money then."

"We can't wait any longer, Joe," insisted the man.

"That loan shark boss of yours can wait one more day," argued Joe.

"We've given you several warnings, Joe," said the man. "Unless you can provide me with the money now, we can't wait any longer."

"Please, just one more day," pleaded Joe.

"We've warned you what would happen," said the man.

"I know, but please . . ."

BLAM!

A bullet burst from the pocket of the man's pea coat into Joe's gut. Blood began to drip onto the fluorescent white snow as the man ran off toward the street. Joe sat his head back as he tried to catch his breath, his body going numb. Lynn, out for her daily jog, heard the gun blast in the distance and rushed in its direction.

As he said those words to me and I said them back, it was probably the first time in my life that it had felt genuine. A man I barely knew dying in my arms who told me he loved me so truthfully you would have sworn we had been married for years. As his body laid there limp in my embrace, his lifeless face nestled into my bosom, his dark black hair with gray sideburns blowing in this cold New York wind, I began to weep uncontrollably. What he said to me played through my head like a song on repeat.

Fate is cruel. This man could have been the one for me, the true love I've been looking for, but I only just met him as he lay dying on a bench in Central Park. I'll never get the chance to take him to dinner, catch a movie, go see a Giants game, or just sit here on this bench with his arm around me.

This bench. This is our bench. And as the newspapers hide his name deep into the obituaries, as the whole world forgets this man and what happened to him, I will hold him deep in my heart as I dream of what could have been on our bench. I will go to his wake. I will speak to his son and try my best to console him with the thought of his father's final moments where he found peace. I'd like to believe Joe would want his son to know that. But I will not tell him of what happened between us. That's for Joe, me, and this bench.

The paramedics took Joe out of my arms. They tried to give him C.P.R. to resuscitate him, but it was no use. They were too late. As they took him away in a body bag and placed him into the back of the ambulance, I couldn't help but say one last thing to this now dead man I had just met.

"I'll always love you, Joe."

Gone

Lowell R. Torres

Marty,

How is life my friend? It's been a while. Too long, and I will take the blame for that. I learned you were back and made no effort to reach out. I know you must have been hurting, and probably still are. You needed a friend and I wasn't there.

I'm sorry.

Now, with that out of the way I think it is imperative to get across the following warning. Even though I'm going to tell you all about it and even though by the end it may sound interesting or intriguing, it is important . . .

No.

It is absolutely VITAL and of the UTMOST URGENCY that you heed these next words:

Don't go into the house. Please do not step foot into the house.

Don't even go near it. Turning onto the weedy dirt track probably means it's too late. Best to just keep driving past, like you do every day. That's why I chose you, Marty. You drive past the thing every day, twice a day, and you could care diddly-freaking-squat about it. I can remember driving past it with you many times and nary a peep. Everyone else I've ever passed by it with has remarked in some way or another about the house, but not you.

Not you, and maybe that means something. Maybe it means nothing. But maybe it means everything.

I feel it. After all these years, I feel the tug the others must have felt. I can hear it calling to me. Maybe it's just the years of psychiatric drugs wearing off, or maybe the noose is now firmly tightened around my neck and it's only a matter of time before I fall. Before I go to the house and step inside. I won't come back out. No one comes back. No one ever comes out of the house.

The damned house.

You know which one I'm talking about, only maybe you don't. I hope to all that is holy that you don't know what I'm talking about. But you have to. It's so obvious, sitting there on Highway 46 just outside of Spencer on the road to Terre Haute. Except maybe you really don't know about it. You don't talk about it, and maybe you don't talk about it because you don't see it. Maybe I'm doing the right thing by sending you this. Maybe I'm saving myself and the others.

Or maybe I'm just damning you along with us.

I know you've at least glimpsed it, sitting there all by itself at the end of the field, just as the land begins to rise into a little forested hill. It's the color that does it; well, that and the size. It's not every day you see a flamingo-pink manse sitting in an Indiana corn field, like someone wanted to build their own personal version of Barbie's plantation house. The columns on the front porch, how can you miss those? And the huge white front door. You've seen that, but you haven't seen the second door, I can guarantee you that partner. You haven't seen the other door, the real front door. The one you may enter but never exit.

I'm sorry. I know I sound like a loon or a maniac or just an idiot. I keep rambling, jumping back and forth. This will all make sense when my story is told. I promise you. You may hate me by then, for what I've done to you. Or you may write this off as the confused writings of a crazy man off his meds. I hope it's the latter. I pray it is.

The house. How can anyone miss the house? It must have been only two or three weeks away from completion when it was abandoned. The paint, vivid pink all over except right under the attic roof. Makes it look a bit like a skull peeking out of flesh.

The pink is faded now but still somehow vibrant. Alive. And the scaffolding is still there, as if a paint crew is going to come finish the job any day. It's hard to miss the little bulldozer sitting next to the house, as abandoned as the old pink bitch, entrenched by decades of growth around it. Or the forklift behind the house, which is a little more difficult to see. It blends in with the trees and the hillside it sits on, but it is there, trust me. It's pointed right at the bitch's ass, like someone meant to drive a couple of metal stakes into her. Only they never did, because there it sits.

I've been close enough to see that no damage has been done to the house, aside from the missing paint at the top. I've been close enough to see that, but no closer. I'm too cowardly to go further. I never actually felt the pull of her until last night, but long before that I knew better than to get too close.

From the road you can still see the stickers on all the windows, but not until you get close can you see that the stickers say those windows were produced by Flodian, Inc. Or that the little dozer reads Percoste instead of John Deere or Caterpillar or even Mitsubishi. Funny thing about those two companies, Flodian and Percoste; they don't exist. Never have.

Just like the house, technically. Mark went to Town Hall, to the zoning office. He spent countless hours scouring the internet. There are no records of the house or of those companies. The people downtown admitted to knowing it exists, but have no files or historical information beyond this one thing: the house and the four acres of land surrounding it are an incorporated area.

The stickers on the window, still perfectly readable after decades of sun, wind, rain and snow, have the date 1951 stamped on them. The newspapers list nothing about the house at any time then or after. Mark found several blacked out passages from June and July of '52 on the microfilm, but the old timers Mark talked to can't, or maybe they won't, remember anything specific from those days. It's like the damned thing just doesn't exist.

Like Mark Evans.

Or Art Holloway.

Becca Coleman.

Richie Hood.

Those names don't ring a bell to you, do they? It's because they don't exist. They never existed. Only they did, Marty. And if you believe any of this you must believe this: those people did exist. They did, but now they're gone.

They were our friends, once upon a time. We had so many good times together. Our week-long camping trips at McCormick's Creek and Timber Ridge; tubing up at Turkey Run; boating out on Monroe Lake; the Golf Cart Wars; playing paint ball; drinking in Richie's barn.

I remember those times like they were yesterday, but I could probably torture you and you still wouldn't know who I'm talking about. Their own parents don't remember them, after all, but I do. Each of them went into that house, Art and Mark by themselves, Becca and Richie together, and they never came out.

It's gotta take some powerful mojo to make it like people never existed. To erase them from memories, pictures, records. Powerful shit, my friend, but somehow I still remember them. Its cause, like you, I'm special too. But my days of being special are done. Finito. I'll stop existing too. I'll be just as gone as them. Hell, I don't even know if you'll get this letter. It might just pop out of existence en route to your mailbox. Gone out of the world like a little bubble of reality, leaving behind a residue that wafts away on the winds of the world.

But my letter might get through. It might. And as far as I know, you still do remember our friends. I haven't really talked to you since the summer after high school graduation. You went off to the Army and the wars; I went off to a life of medication and mental wards. Everyone I know has been convinced that I'm crazy for so long that I mostly believe it myself sometimes.

And maybe I am a little crazy. After all, our friends never would have entered the house were it not for my ranting and ravings. They wouldn't have gone there to try to reassure me that it was just a stupid old abandoned house. Maybe knowing I caused their deaths has made me go a little wacky. Can you blame me? Can you blame me for being torn up over inadvertently murdering my best friends?

My only friends?

I don't think so.

Art wasn't my fault, though. Artie went in there all on his own. I was there, sure, but it was his idea. Artie had been a little off for a few weeks. Not quite himself. Like he was trying to figure out a puzzle in his head, but he didn't know what the puzzle was.

"Hey Greg, you ever . . ." he'd say to me and then drift off and stare into space. I'd ask him to clarify and he'd look at me in a dazed-but-slightly-panicked way, as if he didn't who he was. I didn't pay much attention at the time. I just attributed it to the weed. Art's cousin Jesse had scored a pound of Northern Lights early that summer, and we were high out of minds most of the time.

Artie's disconnect should have triggered some type of alarm in me. He was the most energetic, focused stoner I'd ever known. Always with his notepad and voice recorder, creating and polishing his stand up routine. I could be so high I'd be catatonic and he'd still be going a mile a minute.

Until that June, when his former personality sort of melted away. What was left was someone unfocused, agitated, and often confused. Completely unlike Artie.

I noticed all of this in hindsight, of course.

And really, even if I had reason to be concerned, I doubt I would have said anything. I near worshipped Artie. He could do no wrong in my eyes. Even when his pointed jokes were at their most biting I let the insults slide away. I guess I was in love with him a little bit.

So when he suggested we go get stoned and check out the old abandoned house, how could I say no? When did I ever say no to Art? "Come on, Keller," he goaded when I pretended disinterest. "I only live like a mile away. You can use the exercise big buddy and who knows, we might find some gnarly shit we can sell on like, Antique Roadshow or something."

So that's what we did. I can't tell you why it never occurred to us before. We'd been getting stoned all over the countryside for two years, but we never thought about that house.

I wasn't terribly excited by the idea. You know me, paranoid and scared of my own shadow before I went insane, but I went with little to no arguments. Only, when we got near it I suddenly had to take a leak like you wouldn't believe, so I stopped by the old dozer to piss. Art went on ahead of me.

"Hey, weird," I heard him call out. "Hey Greg, there's another door here. It's, like, in the first door."

That's the last time I ever heard his voice. I heard the grating sound of the door open, like two old bones rubbing together. I heard the door swing shut and its echo, which sounded larger than it should. I didn't hear anything else, only the country night around me, but even that was muted. The chirrups, buzzes and croaks came from a distance. The sounds should have engulfed me, but there weren't any little critters around for at least a hundred yards or more. There was the noise of the occasional car driving by on 46 a quarter mile away, but that was all. I didn't hear Art moving around inside.

Of course I thought he was messing with me. I didn't automatically assume he had vanished without a trace from existence but I didn't feel good about the situation. Something wouldn't let me get close enough to the house to look through the windows. I just couldn't.

What I did was yell out Art's name a number of times. You know how Art could never turn down the chance to talk. But he didn't reply. Even if he were pulling a joke on me, he would have responded at the first sign of concern or alarm in my voice. Finally I told him to go screw himself and I turned tail and ran. I literally ran all the way back to his house. Hell, I sprinted. Yes, you read that right. Fat Greg Keller sprinting through fields at midnight. It would have been funny to me if I weren't terrified. I couldn't explain why I was so frightened, but I was.

When I got back to Art's house I expected him to be sitting on his porch, grinning that stupid shit-eating grin of his. Instead I encountered a cop, Bryce Pickens of all damn people, taking down a report from Mrs. Holloway. When I came out of the shadows she screamed and pointed at me. Being red-faced, sweating like a pig and breathing like a bellows probably didn't help my initial appearance.

"That's him!" she said. "That's the car owner."

"Barb? Everything alright?" I asked. I was too familiar, of course I see that now. But you know how she was always demanding we call her Barb and not Mrs. Holloway or Mrs. H. Hopefully you know.

"Do I know you?" she asked right back. I should have seen the way she looked at me, as one looks at a stranger. I should have known something was wrong and been on my guard, but how could I? How could anyone ever be prepared for something like this?

"It's me, Barb. It's Greg."

That didn't seem to be working.

"Greg Keller, Arthur's friend?"

She kept looking at me like I was crazy. Was she drinking again?

"You're no friend of my husband," she said. She had to be drinking again. I laughed.

"No, your son, Artie."

The look on her face spoke volumes I would examine in my mind for a long time afterward. I knew Barb was lucky to have been able to give birth to Artie. Some rare disease or genetic disorder, the doctors told her before years of therapy and treatments. It's why he was an only child. It's why Barb and Big Art allowed us practically free reign over their house. They wanted a house full of children of their own, but if the closest they could come was Artie's friends, they'd take it.

"I don't have a son," she said with a sob, and turned to the cop. "I don't have a son."

She said that, and it was then that I knew. Not everything, of course. It would be a long while before I could piece together everything. Mark would help me fit together most of the pieces, but Richie and Becca would be gone by then.

It was at that moment I knew something was horribly wrong. Mostly it was the way she grabbed Bryce's arm for protection. That woman hated Bryce Pickens for the mean son-of-a-bitch he was. So many times she and Artie protected me from Bryce and his asshole friends, but now she was seeking Bryce's protection from me.

"Sir, can I see some identification?" Bryce had that look on his face, the look he'd get right before delivering a knee to the thigh or elbow to the ribs. The look of a hunter whose prey had conveniently fallen into his lap.

"I want him off my property, officer," Barb demanded, sadness turning to anger.

"Absolutely, ma'am."

That was it for me. Of all the cops, it had to be Bryce. And the irony, it's still not lost on me. Artie always protected me from the worst that Bryce would have given me in high school, and now Artie wasn't here. Artie had never been here, and this meant Bryce's memory was different. In Bryce's mind, there had never been the crazy practical joker who stopped him and the other jocks from picking on Gross Greg Keller. In Bryce's memory, he had gone through high school treating me as a doormat and despising me not because I had backup, but because I allowed myself to be stepped all over.

I don't like to think of the rest of that night, or the few days after, so excuse me if I skip over the details. Needless to say, I was confused, angry and scared. Can you imagine what it's like to have a completely different set of memories from everyone else around you? From the entire world around you? Even my own parents, who loved Art to death, thought I'd lost it.

And of course, Bryce liberally using his can of pepper spray and charging me with assault on an officer because I demanded answers and wouldn't just get into his car; well, that didn't help. But I didn't spend long in jail. I ended up snapping pretty fast and was transferred over to the Meadows in Bloomington.

Jesus . . . this feeling. The pull, it's like worms crawling inside my head, and the worms have hooks attached. Every time I acknowledge the existence of that pull, every time I allow myself to feel it, another hook catches.

I have to hurry. OK, Marty, we're gonna have to go with the Cliff Notes version.

I ended up at the Meadows, where I was the recipient of enough medication to make a blue whale think it can tap dance on the moon. If electroshock therapy wasn't so frowned upon these days I think they would have just fried my brain and been done with me. Or saved the electric bill and lobotomized me. I was still angry, confused and scared, and I let it show. How can the entire world stop acknowledging the existence of someone? Was I the target of the biggest, cruelest prank in the history of the world, or had I really gone off the deep end?

I had many visitors at first. My parents couldn't stand to see me like that, all doped up or ranting and raving like a madman. For my mom it just confirmed everything she'd ever thought about me. Not only was I fat, but also crazy. You know she'd never been happy with me. It was one thing for my dad to get all bloated as the years went by because she still had memories of Roger Keller: high school and college basketball star. But I was born fat and stayed that way.

Academics were never as important to her as physical accolades, so I was a disappointment from the get go. After the first two visits she stopped coming, but my dad, ever the trooper, maintained a weekly visit for the first several months.

Becca, Richie and Mark would visit. They were my saving grace. Even if they didn't remember Artie and didn't understand why I refused to admit I might be wrong, they were still supportive of me. Well, as supportive as they could be. Maybe a little too supportive. I had been in the Meadows for two months when Becca and Richie decided they would show me the house I had ranted and raved about was harmless. They told me they were going to go and take pictures and videos, so I could see for myself there was nothing wrong. There was no reason for me to be so worried about some dumb old abandoned house.

They should have known better. If I could have just remained calm and explained to them rationally why that would be a monumentally bad idea, things might be different. Instead, I freaked out on them pretty hardcore. The orderlies were forced to make them leave so I could spend the rest of the day in restraints, for my safety of course.

As I'm sure you could now guess, they went to the house. They saw the door, the other door. They entered it. And they stopped existing. Just like that. I felt them leave existence. It was later that evening and I was pretending to be asleep so the orderlies would untie my restraints. Only between one second and the next my restraints were gone. They didn't come untied; they didn't get loose enough to fall off. They were just gone. I had never been restrained, you see, because Becca and Richie had never come to tell me they were going to the house, and I had never flipped out.

The first thing I did was bolt out of bed and run to my dresser, where I had a picture taped up. Originally it was you, me, "Hell's Bells" Teague, Artie, Mark, Becca, and Richie: The Magnificent Seven. The Gone-Away Gang, dubbed so by Richie's dad because we were always heading out of town on some trip or another every chance we got.

The picture was from the camping trip we took in 2006. Remember? Hell's Bells fell into a patch of poison ivy shortly after the picture was taken, and that night, after Artie gave her hell all day, she took a plant and wrote "Jack Ass" on his forehead. It was my favorite picture, detailing the days when we were one of the tightest groups of friends in school. Only now the picture showed just you, me, Mark, and Helen. Becca and Richie were as gone as Arthur had been for two months.

That set my "recovery" back quite a bit of time. Two years, in fact. I basically gave up on life. Either I really had gone insane and the world was conspiring against me, or there was a third, more terrible option. It took me some time to believe something else could be at play. Maybe it was the house, and not me, that was responsible for all of this. But how can a house do that? How can some stupid house make people disappear from existence?

It didn't make sense, and still doesn't. But it's the truth. It has to be. I'm not insane and the world isn't engaged in a cover up to make me appear as if I am. The only other alternative, the only other possibility, is that the house is responsible. Maybe it's alive. Maybe it's a doorway to another dimension. Maybe it's a whole list of things that sound absolutely ridiculous on paper. But I've lived through the last few years, Marty. You have to believe that I'm not just suffering from some horrid delusions. You have to believe I'm not making this all up.

It's what the doctors believed. What else could they believe? What else could I believe? For close to two years I gave up on life. I lay in my bed in my room, or if the orderlies made me get up for the day I would sit in a recliner staring out the window. I didn't want to deal with the present; the present had gone to hell. Instead I spent that time in the past. Reliving memories, days, and events that made me happy. I think that's what eventually got me through. I had the memories of happier times.

Vacationing with Art's family down at Mammoth Cave and Nashville. Hanging out in Richie's barn, getting stoned or drunk on whatever we could get our hands on and thinking we were just awesome because of it. Our countless camping trips. God, do I miss those days. We'd spend weeks out in the woods, just the group of us. I always thought that if we stayed out there forever I'd live happily until the day I died.

Were it not for the memories, I don't know if I'd ever have come back. My dad stopped bothering to write, the doctors stopped scheduling one-on-one time, and the nurses stopped making me get out of bed. I believe they were all waiting for me to die. If it weren't for Mark, I probably would have. I would have just stopped bothering to breathe. But Mark, well, you know how damned persistent he always was. He was like a bulldog with a toy in his mouth, not about to give it up for anyone. I guess I was the toy, because he came to see me two or sometimes three times a week that whole time. Even when I'd just sit there drooling on myself and staring into space, he'd force himself to sit with me for at least thirty minutes. Mark didn't remember Artie, Richie or Becca. His memories had been changed like everyone else, but we were still great friends in them. He'd sit across from me and talk about the times we had. You, me, him, and Helen before she had her accident. I always forgot that, like me, Mark was a loser who lucked into having great friends like you guys.

Only now Artie, Richie and Bec had been erased from existence, you were off in Iraq and Helen was in Seattle. His mom was still an abusive bitch and his dad getting out of prison hadn't helped matters. He was too poor to escape, and too dumb to make it through more than a semester of college. Poor Mark. All he had was me, so he'd visit, hoping that one day I'd snap out of it and join him back in the real world.

I know that's why he did it in the end. The same reason Richie and Becca went out there. He wanted to prove to me that there was nothing wrong with that house. That it was all just my imagination. If he could walk through the house, especially the front door, and video tape the whole ordeal, then I'd have no choice but to see it was harmless. I'd have no choice but to accept that I had suffered from a break in reality and be forced to come back from the brink and join the rat race again. The dumb son-of-a-bitch, he was just trying to help me.

Although I sometimes think maybe that's not the case. Maybe he believed my story. After all, he did all the research on the house and property. He went downtown to talk to people. He dedicated a lot of time to that damned house, and maybe in the end he started to believe. Maybe, in his own way, he was trying to end his own miserable existence. I like to think Mark went there for himself, and not for me.

Regardless, the only part that matters is Mark went to the house. And Mark stopped existing. I woke up in the middle of the night and knew he was gone. I didn't have to check the picture to make sure, because I felt the world was a little lighter. The picture only confirmed what I already knew. There we were. Just you, me and Hell's Bells. I have my arms outstretched, as if each one is around someone's waist, but what used to be Mark and Becca was now just empty space.

That's when I started to feel the call of the house. I had inadvertently fed it too many times and now it was hungry. That's what my mind tells me, but who knows the truth? The only thing I know for sure is that I must now go there. I must face the monster that has destroyed my life and reap the consequences of my actions.

I don't have to tell you that I escaped from Meadows. It wasn't hard. They were so used to me being catatonic that they weren't looking for me to get up and walk out. I changed out of my pajamas into a set of real clothes which hung loose on me, like I was a child playing dress up in his daddy's closet. A lot of people I knew before all this probably wouldn't even recognize me, because I've lost so much weight. The loose clothes were a strange sensation, but they were good enough to get me out of there and not have anyone call the cops as I hitched to my parents house. My bedroom window was still unlocked, allowing me to sneak in undetected long enough to write this letter to you.

Can you believe it, my room is exactly the same as it was the last time I was in it? I expected my mom to convert it into a yoga den or a room for her stupid dogs by now.

But that's it. That's my story, Marty. I'm sorry to have involved you in all of this, but I felt the need to tell someone who hadn't judged me to my face. From the few stories Mark told me about your time in the war I know you have your own demons to worry about. I understand why you never came to visit me. Losing friends is a terrible thing, which is also why I chose to write this to you. You know what it's like to lose people close to you, to lose part of yourself. For you it was a hand; for me it was two years of my life and a healthy chunk of my sanity.

I hope you can forgive me. I hope there's never anything to forgive. I hope this letter simply disappears when I do, or you read it and dismiss it out of hand. But there's another part of me, a very selfish part that hopes you read this and come check out the house. Part of me hopes you'll come join us, but not before sending your own letter to Helen, explaining everything. I both want that very much and dread it with every ounce of my being.

I can only hold onto the thought that when I walk through the door it's not into some unimaginable hell dimension, or into some vacuum in space. It's not hell or heaven or anything like that. I hold onto the thought that when I open that door within a door and walk through, the first thing I'll see is Artie, Richie, Becca, and Mark sitting around a picnic table surrounded by a forest thriving in the heart of summertime. Richie's mammoth sixteen-person tent will be set up under the shade and a fire will be lit, ready for S'mores once the sun goes down. I'll walk through the door and they'll all turn toward me and give a hearty cry of welcome and rejoice. We'll be one step closer to being all together again. Five of The Magnificent Seven, ready to ride out into the sunset together.

With all my heart I hope that's the scene I walk into. God, I hope so.

Take care of yourself Marty. Whatever you decide, whatever you believe, remember the love we all once held for each other. It's what got me through the long lonely nights when all seemed hopeless and lost. It's a powerful magic, love. I hope its powerful enough to defeat whatever it is that awaits me beyond that door.

Your Friend,

Gregory.

Waiting room is to foxhole as confessional is to solitary confinement

from Little Glove in a Big Hand

Tony Brewer

I'm sorry for everything
I never felt I needed to apologize for
until those few moments before
the doctor enters the room.

Light slants through long blinds,
illuminating x-rays of late November
parking lot trees.

His hand is out,
comes to rest on my shoulder.
The words sting like iodine
then soothe like Percodan.

Everything that hurts is waited out.
It builds up till all the truths come out in a fever
that breaks like morning after a long night fighting
over lives that go on no matter who dies
or stays alive in that other room.

This well-lit purgatory works wonders
on mere sons and daughters,
mouths moved by panic.

We lose our footing in the blood,
humorless when instruments are dropped.
Punch drunk where we all at least once
have held each other up against the news.

I run out of places quick to look,
exposed under big lights that never shut off.
Trying to be patient, ready to spill it all,
as if it all is ever going to come out.

I had been prepped for years
but didn't know what to do or say
sitting there waiting,
until I hear my name.
Time to go.
They're waiting for me.

Pigeon Crackers

Thomas V. Nowak

Joey is roaming among the stone foundations of the old bridge and occasionally passes out of sight. "I don't want you going anywhere I can't see you," shouts Mike. "And if a train comes I want you back here at my side." Joey makes a waving gesture to his brother, but doesn't stray far. Joey is eighteen years old and still cannot be left alone.

It is the afternoon of the Fourth of July and hot as an attic and people are sporadically shooting off illegal fireworks throughout the neighborhood. Mike Polachek has neither the mettle nor the enthusiasm to engage in any serious crime but he knows how to make an easy dollar. In late May he and Joey drove to Ohio and packed the trunk of their mother's car with cases of Roman candles, starbursts, M-80s, silver tubes, cherry bombs, and every size of firecracker they could find. Then they drove back to Buffalo where he tripled the price and despite his mother's objections sold as much as he could from the kitchen of her house. This afternoon he bought a case of beer with his earnings and now he and his brother are igniting their surplus of unsold fireworks beneath the bridge that spans the Great Lakes route of the New York Central Railroad.

Mike watches as Joey lights the wick of another firecracker from his cigarette and tosses it into the air. Mike has learned to read the subtle expressions on his brother's face. Most people see only blankness when they look there, but Mike sees the few simple and predictable changes that come and go like the phases of the moon.

Mostly Joey carries a look of confusion, occasionally tempered by some awe. Frequently there is the look of hurt. Rarely Mike sees joy. Today is a rare day, and Joey is excited by the outing beneath the bridge.

The brothers are sitting in an isolated spot where few people go except for the occasional hobo or railroad inspector. Mike takes Joey there frequently. It is one of the few places they can go where they are free of scrutiny. Most adults become suspicious of Joey as soon as they meet him. They instinctively move back a half step and scan him with their eyes when they think no one is looking. They speak to him in simple sentences, if at all. Typically they rotate a few degrees and talk to Mike and ignore Joey entirely except for the occasional glance to assure themselves that he is not about to do something impulsive. But today the two brothers are alone.

It is constantly dark beneath the bridge. It is an ancient iron structure that resembles a pair of muscled shoulders that rest on giant pillars of limestone and crosses over a dozen tracks. No grass grows in its shadow, and even in summer it is as cool as a cave. It is mostly quiet except for the constant hum from the traffic above and interrupted only by the charging rumble of the occasional freight train below. Only that, and the constant cooing from the hundreds of pigeons that for decades have nested among the stone pilings and iron buttresses of the superstructure.

The brothers drink their beer from bottles and smash the empties against the stone pilings. Joey stands up, wipes his mouth with the back of his hand, unzips his fly and starts to urinate out in the open.

"You should at least do that where nobody can see you," says Mike.

"There's no girls here," says Joey. "Nobody can see me."

"I'm here, and I can see. You ought to know better, for crying out loud."

Joey halts his stream, shakes his pelvis and zips his fly. He makes a face at his older brother, but he obeys. A few drops drizzle down the front of his pants. He grabs his crotch and waddles to a corner and urinates against a stone wall. They have been there all afternoon. Mike is sitting on a discarded piece of cardboard with his back propped against a concrete wall. He is four years older than his brother and like their father he is satisfied with quietly sipping his beer and watching. He has even developed a taste for the same brand. Mike resents being Joey's guardian, but as the beer saturates his system the resentment fades and Mike understands why his father drank as much as he did.

Mike waves Joey closer. "I don't mean to yell at you all the time," he says.

Joey nods. "I know."

"It's just that there's trains that come through down here and you could get hurt."

"It's okay," says Joey.

Mike smiles. "Grab another beer."

Joey passes on the beer. Unlike his brother, Joey has never outgrown his fascination with fireworks and his pockets are bulging with firecrackers. He has been lighting them off since early that morning. Hundreds of the things. He has lost interest in simply lighting a firecracker on the ground and watching it explode. He has spent the last several hours drinking beer with his brother and is trying hard to invent new ways to blow off his cache.

Joey is balancing a lit cigarette between his lips. It quivers as the smoke floats about his eyes.He has never learned to smoke and every now and then he sucks air through the cigarette just to keep the embers alive. He reaches into his pocket for a firecracker, lights the wick, and tosses it under an empty bridge girder. It explodes and the boom echoes under the bridge like a cannon. A few dozen pigeons are startled and fly from their roosts.

Joey laughs.

Up to now he has detonated firecrackers under tin cans, in puddles of water, buried them under piles of clay, and dropped them into sewers and manholes. He has shoved them into empty beer bottles, hoping to see the glass explode, but is disappointed when the detonation is muffled and only fills the chamber with smoke. Now he is amusing himself by climbing up the iron girders of the bridge to the undercarriage of the roadway where the pigeons are roosting. The hens sit adamantly on their nests and refuse to scatter even when he comes near. Joey slides a firecracker beneath a nest, lights the wick, and scurries to the ground. The detonation produces a cloud of smoke and pieces of dried grass and leaves float down from the girder. A yellowed smear of yolk dribbles down the concrete pilings. The hen is blown from her nest. She is disoriented and is flying wildly until she smashes into a concrete wall and drops to the ground.

Joey chuckles. The pigeon is stunned and sitting quietly on the ground. He scoops up the bird and returns to his brother who is by now nursing his fourth or fifth beer.

"Look at this," says Joey. "It's too dumb to fly away."

"Big deal," says his brother. "What are you going to do with a dumb pigeon?"

Joey arches his eyebrows and smiles. "Wait." He presses the pigeon to the ground and holds its wings together with his left hand. With his free hand he reaches into his pocket and withdraws a firecracker, and then squeezes the bird's neck until it opens its beak. Joey slides the firecracker into its maw, far down its throat, until it becomes wedged. He lights the wick and waits until the last possible moment before he pulls away.

The pigeon's head explodes and a spray of red and gray curdles fly into the air. The headless carcass sits motionless on the ground. It is still breathing and a small stream of blood percolates from the stump of neck. The bird's torso begins to quiver. Its wings flap once, then again. The carcass stands and begins to walk, its wings still spread. It makes a few steps and then collapses on its side. The small grey thorax rises and falls a few more times, and then the bird dies.

Joey is standing over the pigeon. "Did you see that?"

Mike has been holding his beer bottle to his lips. He is not drinking and is watching his younger brother. "Why did you do that?"

"It just blew the head right off," says Joey.

"You just killed a dumb pigeon. It wasn't bothering you."

Joey is already climbing another iron girder. He realizes he doesn't need to stick a firecracker beneath the resting hen. "They just sit there," he tells his brother as he returns with another pigeon.

"You probably shouldn't be doing that," says Mike.

"Why not? They're just stupid. If you come at them from behind and grab their wings, you can scoop them right out of the nest."

"Just because they're stupid doesn't mean you should kill them. I could probably sneak up on you in the middle of the night and light a firecracker in your ear."

Joey ignores his brother. He has a queer smile on his face as he wiggles another firecracker into the bird's beak. It explodes and he is delighted. He goes back for another pigeon, and then another. Some of the pigeons fly away with the lit firecracker still in their gullet. They explode while the birds are still flying in the air. The wings on the headless carcass keep flapping for several strokes after the explosion until they stop and the bird falls to the ground. This excites Joey even more. Now he tosses each bird into the air as soon as he lights the wick, causing it to fly even higher before the firecracker explodes.

The steady explosion of firecrackers attracts a small crowd of young boys on bicycles. By now there are over a dozen pigeon carcasses heaped on the ground. The boys stand open-mouthed at the edge of the ring of carcasses and watch Joey toss the pigeons into the air. Two boys whisper to each other. They ride away and return with a parent.

"Is this your idea of fun?" says the father.

"They're just pigeons," says Joey.

"There are kids here who are watching you. What kind of example are you setting? You're just killing senselessly."

"They don't have to stay. They can leave."

The man turns to leave. "I'm calling the police," he says.

Some of the boys leave with the parent, while a few stay behind. "I'm not blowing up any more pigeons," Joey tells the small crowd of boys. One by one they turn on their bicycles and ride away. Mike stands up and kicks the pigeon carcasses into a tighter pile and covers them with a piece of cardboard. Joey opens another bottle of beer. "You think the police will come?"

"Maybe," says Mike. "You shouldn't have started with the pigeons. If Pa were still around, you'd get the strap."

"Too late now. Maybe we should go?"

"Where we going to go? The police know who we are and where we live."

The police cruiser turns onto the gravel road that marks the border of railroad property. A police sergeant and his younger partner come out of the car and approach the brothers. They pause as the sergeant uncovers the mound of headless pigeons. The younger policeman spits on the ground, while the other removes his hat and wipes his brow with the back of his hand.

"I see you boys have been amusing yourselves this afternoon," says the police sergeant.

"We've been minding our own business," says Mike.

"Maybe so, but one of your neighbors called in a complaint."

"We're not doing anything illegal. Killing pigeons isn't against the law."

The police sergeant nods towards the pile of headless pigeons. "I'm not sure whether there's any city ordnance about killing street pigeons. But to me it doesn't matter. What you're doing isn't right. I don't need a law to tell me that. Anyway, this is private property, and both of you are trespassing. You need to leave."

The brothers stand up and start walking towards the road. The police officers follow them. "It would probably be a good idea if we drove both of you home," said the older police officer. Then he places his hand on Mike's shoulder. "But I'd like to have a word with you before we go." The sergeant nods to his partner as he escorts Mike behind one of the stone bridge pillars.

"Where is he taking him?" asks Joey.

"They're just going to have a little talk," says the younger officer. "That's all. We can wait for them in the car."

Joey watches out the rear window of the police car until his brother is out of view. "What are they going to talk about?"

"Just things. Issues. Responsibilities."

Mike turns and faces the police sergeant after he releases his grip from his shoulder. "Are you going to beat me?" he asks.

"I knew your father," says the police sergeant.

"Then you know what he would have done. You know how he treated my mother."

"I'm not going to make excuses for the man. He was a good man when he wasn't drinking. I knew him when he was sober. But I didn't bring you back here to talk about your father."

"What then? Killing pigeons isn't illegal. People shoot pigeons all the time."

"It's not about the law. It's about your brother and what he does. He doesn't always know what's illegal or not, and what's the difference between right and wrong. Joey does what you do, or what you let him do."

Mike looks down at his shoes.

"The point I'm trying to make, son," says the sergeant, poking his thick forefinger into Mike's chest, "is that now it's your responsibility. Your father is gone. It's all up to you."

Mike looks up at the police sergeant. His face is already hot from the beer, and now he feels the flush spread across his forehead. "How do you know about my brother?"

The sergeant smiles. "We're the police. It's our job to know. Besides, your brother and your family is no secret. It's a tight neighborhood. Everybody knows."

"So you're saying that what Joey does is now up to me?"

"Basically, yes."

"I take him with me everywhere I go."

"Kind of like a puppy. Is that it?"

"I look out for him."

"Like you did today?"

Mike looks down at the ground again. "Well, we still didn't do anything wrong here."

The police sergeant again pokes his forefinger into Mike's chest. "Actually, you did. Maybe not illegal. But it's not right either." He motions to Mike that their meeting is over and they start to walk back to the police car. The sergeant puts his broad hand on Mike's shoulder. "I want you to know that we'll be watching," he says.

* * *

Most everyone knew that Joey Polachek was "different." His mother never acknowledged the fact and always insisted that Joey was the same as the other boys, but just a "slow learner." But she came close to admitting it one day as she sat sobbing next door with her head in her hands in Adele Slominski's kitchen. Mr. Polachek had gone on one of his binges. He was harmless enough when drunk, usually sliding into a mindless stupor. It was during his rebound that he turned mean and slapped his wife around the house and cursed her for all his shortcomings. After running out of her house on a Sunday morning with a dishrag pressed against a blackened eye and a swollen lip, Rita Polachek had nowhere else to go except to knock on Adele's door.

"You really should leave him," said Adele, packing a towel with ice cubes. "No man has a right to do that to you."

"You're right," said Rita. "I really should."

"Then why don't you?" said Adele, taking the soiled dirt rag from her neighbor's face and replacing it with the cold pack.

"He can beat up on me, or he can beat up on the boys. It's better that he beat up on me."

"He beats your sons?"

"He used to. He hit Joey once," said Rita, sliding the towel from her face. "I never told you this, but that's when I put a stop to it. When Joey was small Emil got into one of his moods. I don't know what Joey did, but Emil smacked him on the side of the head. I don't think Emil meant to hit him as hard as he did, but Joey slept for two days after that. We just couldn't wake him up. Emil realized right away what he had done and he stayed at Joey's bedside the whole time until he woke up. Emil was really sorry for what he did. I put a stop to it right then and there. I told him, no more hitting the boys. If you have to hit someone, hit me, but not the boys. That put a stop to it."

Adele pulled a chair close to her neighbor and grasped Rita Polachek's hands. "You need to move out, Rita. No one should be getting beat up. Not you, not the boys."

"No, no, I couldn't do that. The boys need a father. Emil may not be perfect, but he's still their father and he's a good provider. Emil promised me that he'd never lay a hand on the boys again and he never has. He takes a strap to them when they need it. And when he's not drinking, he's the perfect husband and father."

Rita Polachek wasn't lying. When he was sober, Emil Polachek was almost the kindest of fathers. Each school night after supper after they had cleared the kitchen table he worked with Joey on his reading assignments and arithmetic homework. He did this out of genuine concern for the boy and maybe some out of guilt. Yet try as he might, and despite all of his father's tutelage, Joey never did learn to read on his own and he never learned more than simple addition.

He was physically uncoordinated as well, and what gnawed at Emil was the realization that while his younger son might not ever learn to read or add numbers, he couldn't swing a bat or toss a football worth a dime.

It was Joey's fourteenth birthday, and Rita Polachek had bought Joey a baseball glove. Emil Polachek and his son Mike had gone into the back yard to play catch, while Joey was still in the kitchen finishing his birthday cake. As soon as he was through eating, Joey ran into the yard, the baseball glove already on his left hand. Emil and Mike tossed the ball skillfully between themselves, testing curve balls, knuckle balls, and sidewinders. But Joey just couldn't keep up. He threw the ball wildly, and he just couldn't catch, always chasing the ball into the bushes. After a while Emil lost his patience.

"You play with him," he said to Mike as he tossed his glove onto the grass. "I'll watch."

Emil Polachek returned to his aluminum lawn chair and the case of Miller's High Life and opened another bottle of beer. He sat there watching his two sons, the one who could handle the ball and who, if not athletic was at least confident and capable and showed some promise; and the other, swinging his arm uncontrollably, like a duckling with a broken wing. He took another long swig of beer and waited impatiently for the alcohol to take hold. As he sat there he tried to focus on something other than his two sons playing catch. He noticed some paint peeling beneath one of the eaves of his house. After his sixth or seventh bottle he decided his house needed to be painted. He was able to pull the ladder out of the garage and scrape and prime the peak above the back second story window. Then he fell from the ladder. His boys had long since gone inside and he lay a good for hour at the foot of the house, well beyond dusk, too stunned and too drunk to call out for help or make any sort of noise. By the time Mrs. Polachek came out he was pretty far gone. The ambulance took him to the hospital. He was there for a week and had blood transfusions, antibiotics, and an operation. A blood clot formed in the leg that he injured when he fell. It broke loose and traveled through his veins to his heart where it wedged against the valve. There it grew until his heart tired and exhausted, and then he died.

* * *

As the police car pulls in front of his house Mike Polachek sees the curtains in the front window move. He knows that his mother has been standing there and she has backed away from the window and now is in the living room watching. As the police car pulls to the curb, Mike scans the houses that line the narrow street. Some of his neighbors are sitting on their front porches. They continue their conversations, although he knows they are casting sidelong glances at the police cruiser. It is always a big deal when a police cruiser pulls in front of a house.

The brothers and the two police officers walk to the front door. Mrs. Polachek is waiting. She opens the lock, pushes open the door slightly, and then hurries back into the living room. The police sergeant pulls open the door and they enter the house.

"It's okay, Ma," Joey shouts. "We're not under arrest. We didn't break any laws."

Mrs. Polachek glances at the police sergeant.

"That's right, ma'am," says the sergeant. "There's no arrests today. But we do need to have a word. In private would be best." He nods to the kitchen.

The two brothers sit on the sofa. Mike is quiet. The good feeling that the beer had brought to his system is starting to fade. Joey is squirming next to him on the couch. He bumps his knee against his brother. "I have to pee," he says.

"You need to hold it," says Mike. "Wait until they're done talking in the kitchen."

Joey squeezes his thighs together and starts to rock on the sofa. The younger police officer stands at the opposite end of the living room and watches the two brothers. Mike smiles on behalf of his brother and the police officer nods. Mrs. Polachek and the police sergeant return to the living room. As soon as they enter Joey scurries past them into the kitchen towards the bathroom. Rita Polachek thanks both of the police officers and shakes their hands. She latches her front door after they leave and then stands back from the front window and watches the police cruiser until it pulls away from her house. Then she sits down on the sofa opposite to her son Mike. She drops her face into her hands and begins to cry.

Joey returns to the living room and sits next to his mother. "Why are you crying, Ma?" he asks. "The police are gone and we're not under arrest."

Rita Polachek doesn't answer. She just shakes her head and puts her arm around him. Joey lays his head on his mother's shoulder.

"Have I been such a bad mother?" she asks.

"It's not you, Ma," says Mike.

"What is it then? Is it too much to ask you to keep an eye on your brother? " Rita Polachek reaches around her son Joey and pulls him closer. "What's in your pocket?" she asks.

Joey sits bolt upright and his eyes grow wide. "I'll show you." He opens a few buttons in the front of his shirt and pulls out a ball of crumpled newspaper. He lays the package on the coffee table. The newsprint is stale and yellowed.

"It's filthy," says Rita Polachek. "It doesn't belong in the house, much less inside your shirt."

"You just wait, Ma." Says Joey. "You'll see." He delicately unwraps the package as if it were a fine birthday present. He steps back from the coffee table as he pulls back the last sheet of newsprint.

"Oh," says Rita Polachek as she covers her mouth with her hand. She looks at Joey. Then her eyes stop at Mike. "Why," she says, "why did you let him bring it home?"

The pigeon carcass is stiff and the feathers are matted. It has no head, just a clean crater the size of a quarter where the head should have been. A small collar of blood stains the newsprint.

"Never seen anything like it, have you, Ma?" says Joey with some pride. "The firecracker took the head clean off." For the second time that day Mike sees joy in his face.

Rita Polachek lifts her hands before her, fingers spread, as if she is trying to push the room away. "Remove it," she says. "Just remove it from my house. I don't want to see it."

"Ma, they shoot pigeons all the time. What's the big deal?"

Rita Polachek doesn't even glance at Joey. "Just remove it," she says. "Get it out of my house."

No one in the room is moving. Finally Mike kneels at the coffee table and wraps up the pigeon carcass. He hands it to his brother. "Let's go," he says. "We'll get this out of here." They head for the front door.

"And don't drop it anywhere around the house or in the street," says Rita Polachek. "I don't want any of the neighbors to see it."

Mike and Joey walk down the sidewalk. Joey is holding the pigeon carcass. "You'd better put that inside your shirt," says Mike.

"What are we going to do with it?"

"Drop it somewhere where no one will find it. You'd better not blow up any more pigeons."

"I guess I won't anymore. Ma's mad."

"It's my fault. I should have stopped you from blowing up the pigeons."

"I still don't get it."

"So what. You may never get it. There are some things that I don't even get. It doesn't make any difference. You just need not to do it."

Mike slips a glance at Joey. He is wearing the hurt face. "It is hard for you sometimes, isn't it?" says Mike. "I mean knowing what to do, and when."

Joey nods. "It wouldn't be bad if someone told you ahead of time what to do. If they gave you directions. Now people just get mad, or they look at you funny, or they just ignore you."

Mike puts his arm around his brother's shoulder and grips his shoulder. He feels the newspaper inside his brother's shirt crumple against his side. "Just keep that package hidden," he says. "For now, those are my directions." Joey smiles.

Mike glances back at his house and sees the curtains in the front window move ever so slightly. He doesn't see his mother, but he knows she is there, standing and watching. It has been well over an hour since his meeting with the police sergeant below the bridge and he still feels the uncomfortable prodding of the man's thick finger in his chest. Mike looks down the street at the other houses on the block. It is a narrow street, barely wide enough for two cars to pass, lined on either side with rows of monotonous clapboard houses that crowd the road like overbearing foreheads. It has started to drizzle and the people on the front porches have gone inside to escape from the rain. He thinks some of the front curtains are moving. He can't see the people behind the curtains, but he imagines they are there, furrowed brows and all, watching.

Bought the house for the yard

Joey Minutillo

If you asked Ken why he bought the split-level ranch
on the corner of Delwick,
he'll clear his throat and say the yard.
Do you see this yard? Weedless.
That willow bends over like it's telling you a secret.
I saw that, I saw the birdbath, I saw the grass
cut like the pattern of a quilt and had to buy it.
Paid cash. Went and filled the shed with top-tier trimmers
and sprays you had to use gloves with. I bought a zero-turn
before a new furnace. December came, I shuddered.
But the lawn was healthy.

As Ken sat cross-legged on the sidewalk,
house smoldering from the inside out,
the first thing that came to mind
was how he was letting the yard go.
Six dandelions. Two by the tulips with weak stems,
three in the mulch by the birdbath,
and one that looked like the moon
between slabs of walkway.

The hedges needed attention. Bed head in all directions,
green steel wool sitting wet behind the sink.
There were yellowed spots near the mailbox

from the neighbors Jack Russell doing his business every
morning at seven.
He used to chase him off with a paintball gun
but as his third summer on Delwick rolled towards September,
he found himself enamored with installing
central air in the garage.

Ken watched the roof over the living room buckle.
It'd been around fifteen minutes since he'd
made it through the screen of gray to watch his house
turn into a rut. Neighbors began collecting in the road,
Children bundled in strollers, the Jack Russell heeled on a leash,
hoping to yank his owner towards the dead patch.

A fire engine roared into the cul-de-sac. It emptied.
"Keep a safe distance folks, a safe distance. Back here,"
the largest fireman flocked a group behind a manhole.
The glow from inside of the house weakened.
Wood splintered over the voices of neighbors jawing.
Everything blanketed in soot, flat and shapeless.
Everything Nebraska flat. His house was now the yard.

The Effects of Alphabet Soup

Joey Minutillo

The can is white and red stripped
like a barber's pole with plain
green text that reads
First Choice Alphabet Soup.
This is lunch, along with
a slice of dry whole wheat bread
and limeaid.

I take the handle of a can opener
and peel the lid back so it folds
over and touches the side of the can.
Ds and Ms float in the condensed broth
like islands of sand, pushing the parsley
and chunks of chicken like volcanic waste.

Spelling words in alphabet soup
is hard. Never enough vowels,
too many Xs. I spelled 'cartwheel'
at lunch one time in grade school.
My friend Francis couldn't read well.
I wonder if he understood alphabet soup.

Alphabet soup is powerful. It turns
spoons and the sides of a bowl
shaped like a turtle's shell
into a piece of paper. Paper
that spells words like *fuekfl*
and *throlx*. This is where
Dr. Seuss got his genius.

JOIN NOW!

Jesse K. Cox

Jonathan stood in front of the full-length mirror screwed to the back of his bathroom door. With both hands he pinched, then folded, his pudgy hirsute belly. The thirty-six-year-old man did this every day after a steamy shower. This was after bracing himself against the shower's granite tile and brushed metal rail to masturbate, less for the pleasure and more as part of a necessary daily routine.

Jonathan looked himself up and down, imagining the old days. In high school, he'd used his firm, muscular body to terrorize other teenage boys on the football field, ferociously hurling them to the turf to the cheers of his hometown. The people adored Jonathan Elish so much his number fifty-two hangs in the school's gymnasium, although he worried the red and white jersey would be lost in the move to the new, bigger high school building situated among corn and soybean fields on the city's outskirts.

Most people thought Jonathan had what it took to go big. He had an NFL body, and the only requirement to take the next step would have been a quick stop in East Lansing to play college ball at Michigan State. Jonathan had a major league pitching arm, but stuck with football because of the girls—it was always for the girls. Nobody really gave a shit about high school or college baseball; people cared more about the quarterbacks he knocked out more than batters he struck out. Football ruled North Hamlet's imagination as much as basketball. It was Indiana, after all.

The full-length mirror aroused a conflict of contempt and gratitude in Jonathan every day. His landlord, a taciturn Greek immigrant who bore a peculiar odor of steamed broccoli and cinnamon, put the mirror there. The spindly old man, whose rapid metabolism Jonathan coveted, believed everyone should see themselves fully cleansed. Jonathan hated not seeing his receded mushroom penis, which hid under the folds of his doughy, alabaster midsection, but he could always remember the better days. He saw in the mirror the days in the locker room, when his monolithic pecs and biceps twitched and flexed and a towel cracked across a spindly freshman's bare, pink ass.

"If I work at it, I think we've got a shot," he said, patting his belly like an obedient Labrador. "We just need to be a little more active, really go out and get the blood flowing."

He cupped the loose flesh around his thigh and gave it a shake, then pulled it tight. He squinted, tilting his head left, then right, looking for any sign of muscle.

"Yes, indeed. A little activity and we're back in business," he said, flexing his biceps and delighting in the lumps that formed between his forearms and shoulders. "Son-of-a-bitch, it's time for a comeback."

Jonathan rushed to the front door of his one-bedroom, one-bath second-floor apartment for the daily newspaper. It was Sunday, so every opportunity in North Hamlet would be splashed in four-color glory from the front page to the classifieds. Overwhelmed by inspiration, Jonathan failed to dress himself before stepping into the hallway. He realized his mistake and retreated, embarrassed and now paranoid, behind the heavy aluminum door. He worried people would see him for what he is, not what he used to be.

Instead of dressing himself, Jonathan grunted and huffed as he stretched his hairy, sausage fingers in vain. The paper was just too far.

"Jesus Christ, I pay for home delivery—to my fuckin' home!" he bitched to himself. "I'm gonna have to write damn letter and give these sons-of-bitches a piece of my mind."

Jonathan could write a letter. He despised the unfair stereotype of the dumb jock. Math never turned out well, but composition, the manipulation of words into bold ideas, that's where he excelled.

Writing a letter of complaint, he couldn't pass up the opportunity to impugn the sloppy work of others.

"I'll get to that later," he said, staring at the newspaper, assessing the situation.

He rejected the idea of dressing himself just to retrieve his paper. Walking fourteen paces down the short, barren hallway to the brown, particle board dresser in his bedroom was a step toward the activity he sought. He weighed four hundred seventy-two pounds, which meant a one-way trip would burn three calories. By the time he had clothed himself and retrieved the paper—unexposed—twelve calories would be spent. But Jonathan detested the idea of bending to the lazy will of a subpar newspaper employee.

"It's the principle of the matter," he reasoned with no one in particular.

Closest to the door inside his apartment sat a six-inch television remote on the brown, particle board coffee table he'd clumsily assembled a year ago. The screws gave him the most trouble, as his swollen digits fumbled and fretted for almost three hours. He burned fifty-six calories, though.

Crusts of old, dried food flaked off the esoteric remote buttons. In five years of owning the television remote, Jonathan only used five buttons: channel up, channel down, volume up, volume down and power. He contented himself in never finding out the exact purpose of the buttons.

For every time he extended the remote toward the television and squeezed the black rubber pad, a quarter of a calorie dropped away, but was quickly replaced by dozens more when he shoveled the next handful of corn chips into his mouth.

Jonathan extended the remote, this time to reach for the paper in his hallway. He braced his knee against the door jam and leaned out as though a false move would send him hurtling into the hallway abyss. The remote tapped and slipped off the paper's plastic bag.

"Don't know why they bother covering the damn paper," he muttered. "Not like the forecast called for showers in the hallway."

He tried everything, lunging, poking and slapping, each effort only pushed the folded paper farther away. With a final lunge, the remote slipped away from his kielbasa fingers, skidding past the newspaper.

"God-damn-it-son-of-a-bitch-motherfucking-piece-of-shit!" he ranted, then covered his mouth as the epithet echoed off the other white, aluminum doors with gold numbers. Jonathan, his breath labored and stammering, slumped back into the apartment.

"There's got to be a better way," he pondered, tugging his scrotum out a sweaty fold in his thigh. Then he saw it: the afghan.

Jonathan's grandmother crocheted the blanket when she was a teenager. That's what people did before television and the Internet reduced the country to a consortium of diabetic compulsive masturbaters and failed dreamers. Only some of the outrageous, idiot teenagers with freakishly high metabolisms held celebrity status. Once they fattened up—if they hadn't killed themselves for the sake of good television—they retired to a sedentary lifestyle in which the act of burning calories was tax deductible. Second-floor apartments such as Jonathan's were automatic write-offs, assuming the tenant burned calories taking the stairs and not riding the elevator.

The incentive program seemed a progressive step in improving universal health care when Congress unanimously ratified it. The day scientists revealed vigorous masturbatory sessions burned as many as one hundred calories at a time, the entire system collapsed. The tax loophole and the rest of the nation's social programs made it possible for most Americans to make money doing nothing at all. As for the people, those who worked found themselves irrevocably in debt under the massive tax burden.

People had a choice to turn off the televisions and computers and pitch in. There was always a choice. They simply needed to unplug themselves and ask for a job anywhere, but the prospect of daytime television and federally funded orgasms proved too attractive to pass up.

Police arrested Jonathan at a football party with a kilo of cocaine on the coffee table in front of him, powder all over his nose. Not to mention the breasts of what would turn out to be an underage co-ed on the couch next to him. It was the best thing that ever happened to him. He served two years in state prison before the governor's budget cuts left the prison shorthanded and led to his early release.

With no job, or expectations of one, the world was full of opportunity. Much like the newspaper he now coveted.

Jonathan lumbered to the front of the couch, weaving his fingers into the afghan's blue, red, and yellow threads.

"That's what I'm talkin' about," he said triumphantly, lashing the blanket across the living room like a lasso. "Just like the rodeo."

He waddled back to the half-open door and investigated the hall for traffic. "I gotcha now, you little son-of-a-bitch," he said, poking his tongue out the corner of his mouth.

The first attempt sailed left and the second whipped right, but Jonathan had the paper's coordinates locked in now. Drawing it back slowly, Jonathan lashed the afghan precisely as the phone on the coffee table near his head chirped an ear-shattering tone. Startled, his hand released the blanket at the apex, launching it down the stairwell at the end of the hallway.

Another tirade of muddled vulgarities known only to Jonathan erupted from his snaggletoothed mouth. He answered the phone on the third ring.

"What?" he said, making clear his irritation and yanking his coarse, sandy hair. "You sons of bitches have the nerve to call me on a Sunday and ask how my service is? Balls, big balls, my friend."

The voice on the line responded with a higher tone of consolation, but not enough for Jonathan. His once-chiseled chest, which was now just two sagging bags of fat, jiggled in exclamation as he barked into the phone.

"The son-of-a-bitch delivery jackass tossed my paper down the hall, nowhere near my door!" Jiggle. "No, I am not pleased with that cock-sucking jackass just flinging my paper every which way!" Jiggle-jiggle-jiggle.

Jonathan Elish's newspapers usually sat in a pile on his doorstep every morning, tripping him when he ventured out for another case of beer, his disability check, a fresh cardboard pallet of corn chips, or the latest interactive pornographic video at Ned's Beaver Hunt on Calumet Avenue. In a fit of rage, he gathered up the papers and heaved them into the community trash chute near the stairwell once a week. This remarkable activity spike burned three hundred calories or more, depending if he stopped at the bank to cash his disability check, which would be spent on corn chips, beer, and the latest interactive pornographic video.

"I'm not saying I didn't get my paper," he said evenly. "It's that it wasn't properly delivered." Jiggle-jiggle.

This particular paper never found its way to Jonathan Elish's doorstep because the delivery woman, a fifty-five-year-old, four hundred fifty-pound diabetic, keeled over dead in the hallway early that morning. Jonathan's neighbor, thirty-four-year-old Althea Trowbridge, a quarter-ton diabetic, wheeled her extra-wide wheelchair into the hallway for a brisk roll to the stairway and back. She truly exercised because she'd never learned to masturbate and found the whole idea of touching herself "down there" repugnant and unladylike. Trowbridge spotted the delivery woman—whom paramedics were later too winded to identify and subsequently tagged her as a Jane Doe—and called the police to file a complaint.

The report, as it would appear in Monday's crime blotter, read:

"A woman from an apartment complex in the 3200 block of Cline Avenue reported an unidentified woman impeding her daily exercise routine. Police filed, but later rescinded, charges of vagrancy and public nuisance against the Jane Doe, whom paramedics later pronounced dead."

Jonathan slept through squawking sirens and heavy footfalls of police and paramedics waddling in and out of his building.

"It's just the principle of the matter." Jiggle-jiggle. "Put that on your shit bag survey." Jonathan slammed the phone into the cradle, pleased with the manner in which he'd solved the matter. He prided himself on being a problem solver.

Without the afghan, his needed those brilliant problem-solving abilities more than ever. He jiggled and wheezed to the front of the couch then collapsed into the two crater-like dips in the cushion. Sitting always helped him think, and the solution was out there. He'd just have to masturbate on it, a method from which he derived most conclusions. When he reached for the television remote to turn on one of the seventy-five federally funded adult movie channels, his expectant hand found nothing but a graveyard of corn chip wrappers and mounds of yellow crumbs.

"Aw, son-of-a-bitch!" he shouted, remembering the hallway had swallowed the remote, too. "Doesn't matter anyway."

Jonathan hadn't masturbated in a seated position in nearly 12 years, not since prison. The endless sea of rippled fat made it physically impossible. He had to do it standing up in the shower, an act burning one hundred seventeen calories.

To assist his brainstorming, Jonathan shoved a pencil in his bare navel, watching it teeter back and forth like a lunatic's yellow clock hand. He grabbed a few more pens and pencils from the rickety brown coffee table. He neatly wedged each tip between the rolls of fat until his entire billowing abdomen was a giant, mutant porcupine.

"Son-of-a-bitch, this is madness," he said, slapping his chubby hand against the couch's green twill armrest in defiance.

He rocked and grunted, straining against the pens and pencils stifling every bend of his body. Angling himself on one hip, a few writing utensils falling away, he slipped to a knee on the floor and shed the rest of the multicolored pens and yellow No. 2's. This burned at least ten calories, but Jonathan decided the act merited no encore.

Standing, but a little lightheaded, Jonathan walked to the front door and cracked it, scouting the hall shadows. The drab yellow light shined all clear, and Jonathan took a deep breath.

"This is it," he said, slicking the blond swatch on his head, which immediately sprang back. "Desperate times call for desperate measures, and I'm a desperate man."

Jonathan Elish was desperate, but it troubled him that he could not remember why. He hesitated at the thought but let it pass; more important things remained ahead.

He snorted and winced, attempting to stretch his atrophied hamstrings. Reaching forward, he would swear those were toes he saw—yellow, infected toenails capping hairy knuckles. This stoked his excitement, like those Kentucky Derby horses in the stalls before the race. He felt sorry for the horses now. The jackass teenagers with high metabolisms turned the event into an equestrian demolition derby. Jonathan never agreed with the change, but he and the rest of the population were powerless to do anything about it.

"At least we'll have glue," he told himself every spring.

Jonathan braced himself in the doorway, mere feet from the newspaper.

"It's go time," he said.

In one lurch, the entire mass of his jiggling, bare body darted out the door, exhilarating Jonathan more than the palm of his hand ever had. He felt like a teenager, imagining himself back on the football field, crashing toward the quarterback.

"You're mine now, you son-of-a-bitch," he bellowed as the newspaper sat, showing no signs of intimidation.

Standing over the thick newspaper wrapped in clear plastic, Jonathan victoriously pumped his arms and knelt to scoop his prize.

And then a gasp.

"Sweet Jesus, Mr. Elish," a shrilled woman's voice called, shredding his celebration to confetti. Blood rushed to his head and Jonathan peered upside down through a narrow window framed by his dimpled thighs and scrotum, and he saw just the wheel of Althea Trowbridge's chair. Jane Doe's collapsing in the hall hampered her tax deduction plans, and this was the moment she'd chosen to make up for it

From Althea's chair, she saw only slabs of pale, bruised meat holding up an enormous, fuzzy, wrinkled asshole.

The idea of retreat occurred to them in the same moment. Althea threw her hands forward, launching the wheelchair backward. Jonathan exploded toward his gaping apartment door.

Each foot bare foot crashed into the unforgiving, thinly carpeted floor, paced with a "sonofabitch-sonofabitch-sonofabitch."

Jonathan focused on the white aluminum door in front of him, and was momentarily surprised when the door turned black and full of stars. He had a second to realize he had just run face-first into the doorframe before he lost consciousness and dropped in a heap.

The pudgy man awoke face-down, and his head pounded, his chin stung, and his nose ached. He rolled onto his side, noticing the door hung ajar. He wondered how many people rolled past his massive dimpled posterior without a word or call for help. From his hip, he hooked a heel on the door and slammed it closed against the cushy weatherstripping, sealing the apartment with a pop. The newspaper's plastic cover crinkled in his palm, and he grinned proudly at his prize.

Coming to a knee, Jonathan crawled to the green tweed couch and collapsed in satisfaction. Shucking the paper from its plastic, he flipped through the A section, then B section, then C section until he found the Join Now! section. The colorful insert, a federally funded project, had every club happening and activity in the area. He took one of his porcupine quill pens and held it, ready to circle.

"Competitive eating," he read aloud, sneering when he discovered it was only hot dogs. "Son-of-a-bitch, I hate hot dogs. What's wrong with pies or corn chips?" Jonathan craved cherry pie; he could eat it all day if it weren't so damn expensive.

His eyes scanned and jumped to the next page, turning up gardening clubs, cooking classes, Bible study groups, team pool wading leagues, team masturbation, fart choirs, and, curiously, a two-week fantasy employment camp in a local automotive factory. None of those appealed.

"Competitive staring," he read with intrigue. "For teams and individuals, this league meets Tuesdays and Thursdays. Join Now!"

The idea rolled around his brain for a moment. His hand started toward the phone when it recoiled and he said, "Nope, Tuesdays and Thursdays are no good.

"Maybe there will be something better next week." He yawned, "Son-of-a-bitch."

Jonathan Elish tossed the coveted Sunday edition of the North Hamlet Herald over the side of the couch—where he inevitably would trip over it—closed his eyes, and took a nap.

Just a Cold

Keoni Hooker

I don't like fire.

I never have. As a kid it always reminded me of the devil and all the scary things that were under my bed. But I've always found it hypnotizing. Whether you're watching the smoke spiral and twist above the flames from a distance, or pissing yourself because of the eye-melting proximity you are to it, you just can't look away sometimes. Kind of like a car wreck.

So when, at approximately 10:23 that morning, a red Toyota Camry was split in half by a speeding taxi cab, I couldn't shut my eyes. The Toyota seemed like it was void of a driver, though it was hard to determine from my window perch. Yet, as fast as the taxi driver was driving and meandering around the road, he couldn't be blamed for the tragedy. He was too busy reaching behind his seat and attempting to deal with an aggressive and unruly passenger, an act that resulted in a vicious mess of blood, metal and smoke involving both vehicles, in the first floor of the office building.

I've been watching the flames crawl up the building for hours now, after the consequential explosion of the wreck, and am perplexed at how my window hasn't melted off my wall. Every once in a while the view is interrupted by a person, usually performing a complicated version of the "holy crap I'm on fire" salsa, who decides that falling silently to the pavement below is a better option than finishing their dance. Sometimes, I see someone bloodied, flailing their arms and screaming for help, only to be dragged back in by some unseen force, never finding their exit. I wish I could tell you that this was the most disturbing event I'd witnessed in my life. Hell, even in the past few days. But it's not.

The worst images have come from, as usual, the TV. But not in a Hollywood-produced, "overpaid screaming actor" way. There's no one twisted enough on this Earth that could reproduce the footage I've seen from the news reports in the past few days. The atrocities that have been committed and captured by unfortunate cameramen have been so severe, I'd like to think that God has a special place in hell for these common people that violate even the most basic of human rights. But I also don't think God is here for this special occasion. A verdict I decided on after yesterday.

The Secretary of Education was the star of a "late-breaking news coverage". She opened the press conference by stating that she was now the highest ranking member of the United States Government. It was never mentioned what had happened to our President, Vice President, or any of the other 13 members of the presidential cabinet that ranked above her, but based on the way she was shaking and the blood on her dress, I thought she maybe had a clue.

Her skin made me think of a moldy egg. A pale, sick-white, cracked canvas with raised, green hills sporadically spread every where amongst it. As her hands shook with obvious fear, she informed me and the rest of the nation that a State of Emergency had been placed on the country, and that Martial Law had been officially declared. After a room full of reporters finally quieted down, she talked for another 30 minutes, about quarantines, cooperation, and a foreseeable end to the madness, but at that point, I could only understand ten minutes worth of it.

She kept mumbling to an incoherent degree, then re-articulating her words for the entire speech. Part of that might have been my fault, but it didn't matter anymore. This news, combined with the footage I'd seen earlier of a cameraman watching helplessly as a woman was torn apart by a pack of children, confirmed that I wouldn't be turning the TV on anymore.

I'd been feeling a little down and out for a few weeks. Nothing serious, just the usual allergy and weather afflictions I've been suffering off and on for most of my life. Three days ago it turned into a full-blown cold. Nothing serious, but if it's one thing I hate more than the 80's, it's getting people sick. More than that, I certainly didn't need my weak immune system out in the open with whatever was making people violently ill at my office. People had been calling off all week with the term "explosive" and "Crippling" used more than enough warrant a day off. When I called my boss to inform him I wouldn't be able to come in, he did his best to cover his suspicion that the entire office had secretly gotten together to screw him over.

"Been goin' around." he said.

I tried to watch TV, but all my favorite shows were being interrupted by a news bulletin of some kind, highlighting some new tragedy. A train full of pedestrians derailing and exploding for no apparent reason interrupted my court shows. A change of the channel produced a daytime talk show, lighthearted and right down my alley. I settled in for some fluff, only for "Good Times with Parker and Carol" to be replaced ten minutes later by a "News 10 Special Report!" The scene was a traffic jam, not really that major a deal in the city, but this traffic jam was different. A brawl between a few dozen people had broken out. They were climbing over their cars, dragging bystanders out windows, biting and kicking and clawing. I even saw the flash of gunfire a time or two and what looked like a maniac wielding a baseball bat. My body informed me that sleep would be more beneficial than divulging in this break down of social norms.

That night, I woke up wondering if the cold pills I took were actually cyanide. The NyQuil and flu medicine I had taken were doing nothing to stop this illness from rampaging through my system. After exporting all foreign and domestic fluids in my body to the Greater Porcelain Domicile, I sat against my bathroom wall, wiped of any and all power to do much else. Using the sink as support, I got to my feet and turned the faucet on. After a splash of water and second wave of over-the-counter drugs, the pale, dripping face in the mirror revealed the ugly truth that I should get out more. Sick or not, no one is this pale.

According to the clock, and the intense but clear signals from my stomach, I hadn't eaten in a whole day. The kitchen suddenly became a very welcome site. I riffled through the fridge, quietly praying that each item I picked up would seem appealing. The steaks I bought recently looked inviting, but I had no patience for cooking. There was some applesauce, but I knew it wouldn't help either my cravings or my sickness. Not wanting to take anymore time looking or standing, I settled for some TV on the couch with some chicken noodle soup and crackers.

The news was still going, reporting on more and more violent crimes springing up randomly on the city. I was more interested in how the bowl of soup in my hand had been replaced with flavorless drivel, yet smelled like a backyard cookout. With each bite, the too-hot liquid coursed through my body, yet had the flavor appeal of Kool-aid without sugar. The only taste that made me smile was when my tongue hit the bottom of the spoon. I sucked every drop of broth off the concave utensil, enjoying the caustic taste of liquid on steel.

Putting the bowl on the table in disappointment, I wiped my hands free of crumbs when I noticed how bumpy and irregular the task had been. I searched my head, but could find no way to explain how 2nd degree burns replaced the smooth surface of my left palm. I ran to the bathroom on instinct and blasted the cold water on as high as it would go. When one of the vessels popped and seeped puss and blood from the open wound, my mouth mimicked the process, using the just-consumed food as a substitute liquid for the demonstration.

I wrapped my hand slowly with a towel. Not because it hurt, mind you, but because that's as fast I could move. After taking more cough syrup, I retired to my bedroom, convinced that, not only would I have a good day at work, but that I'd have a funny story to tell when I got there. About how I got second degree burns and didn't even know it.

The next morning I laid in bed and watched the sun rise. My alarm clocked blinked and blared at me for at least half an hour, but I couldn't bother to shut it off. I could only think about two things: the fact that my boss was going to be upset with me for not coming in, and whether he would believe me when I told him I felt like my bones had been replaced by jagged, rusty metal poles. The impossible stiffness of my body made sure that the newly forced, shuffle-based movement to the phone took unnecessarily longer than it should have, while several calls to my work, resulting in a busy signal, proved my efforts to be pointless.

The walls graciously helped me along to the living room, where I hoped the TV would offer some kind of release from the misery that was dominating my being. I felt numb. As if all of my limbs were asleep and every cell in my body took their cue from them. I knew I was significantly sicker than yesterday, proven by the involuntary brain signals my body chose to ignore. Signals like "swallow" or "clench the muscles". Further proof came when I sat down and found out I had sat in something . . . Squishy. I stood up to see a light-brown and red stain on the cushion. The problem was that there wasn't enough of it on the couch itself to merit the sensation I had just felt when sitting down. When a pat to my butt resulted in the same squishy effect I had seconds earlier, I decided not to investigate any further.

I moved slowly back to my room, not wanting to get any of the excrement on the floor. I wasn't sure I'd be able to get back to my feet if I had to get down to clean it up. After cleaning myself to the best of my ability, I put on some new sweatpants and made my way to the phone. Crapping yourself without knowing it normally means you need help. I tried to call my parents. Then my sister. Then the hospital. But all the lines were down or busy. I tried to call my phone company to see why they decided to torture me today, of all days, but they wouldn't pick up either. Disgusted with myself and the pathetic service the phone company was providing, I decided to put my faith in the TV for an escape from all this disappointment.

Aside from the random commercials, it appeared every single channel had dispatched a news team of some kind. The reports were varied from station to station, but all of them contained scenes that were simply too intense to seem real. I found one with headlines scrolling at the bottom and tried to catch up on the days tragedies, but was denied due to a lazy or dyslexic Teleprompter Operator. Three stations later, it seemed the same Operator was working for a different network, only he managed to distort the DOW ticket scroll as well. Every station, it seemed, hired this one person, or perhaps union of people, to do nothing but place unintelligible fonts and shapes on the screen.

I broke one of the end tables in my clumsy, yet frenzied rush to the computer for answers.

I began to grow concerned that the teleprompter conspiracy had grown too large when my Google homepage appeared to be constructed of unreadable symbols and markings. Their tactics incited pure rage when every page I surfed through for the next few hours mocked me with illegible scratches. It was all too much. First, I get singled out by the phone company. Then, the TV people have it out for me. Now, these same bastards, it appeared, had put a virus on my computer. I could envision them, mocking me behind my computer screen while I searched, desperately, for answers. I made a fist and reached into the screen as hard as I could to silence them. As I picked the glass out of my hand, I felt confident that the possible group of terrorists that were torturing me with indecipherable figures everywhere I turned would no longer be able to get their giggles from my frustration.

A crimson streak danced on the wall in my hallway, painting the path to my bathroom, where I was washing my mangled hand. As the blood and glass splattered and chased each other down the drain, I stared into the mirror, mystified, at the newly formed green pustules that were inhabiting my face. I desperately wanted to know what these uninvited, moss-covered blotches of skin felt like, but a Poke and Prod investigation technique is only useful when your fingertips feel sensation. A more forceful, irritated approach resulted in gaping hole in my cheek. My teeth ground off a layer of enamel in fury. To this moment, I still don't know whether the blood on the shattered remains of the mirror is from my wounded cheek or my forehead.

I made my long way back to the living room, collapsing on the couch in despair. Everything in my gut told me not to trust the TV again, but I needed to find out why 911 was unreachable. Conspiracies withstanding, I should be able to call 911 from anywhere. I searched for hours, ignoring any scrolling words and staring directly into the middle of the screen while flipping past anything that didn't look like a man or woman, sitting at a desk, talking directly to the camera. However, each discovery of a trusted news anchor showed them in a shaken, sweating state. And every one of them, it seemed, had problems with mumbling.

Or perhaps it was an audio error, caused by a vengeful or stupid studio technician. Whatever it was, I could only hear them half the time.

Then, without warning, the camera switched to a view of a woman, standing at a podium. She pulled at her hair nervously, producing a handful of locks. The audio was messing up at the station again, so I turned the channel, but she was on every one of them. All the stations were broadcasting her. As I was soon to find out, our new, hours-old president was about to tell us that our society was ready to come tumbling down.

Beethoven's "Moonlight Sonata", while admittedly an eerie choice given current circumstances, remained one of my favorite pieces of music on the planet, due to it's calming effect on me, regardless of what mood I was in. At this point, I needed something to listen to other than my rapid heart beat. I watched my window as society ripped itself apart by the limbs while the perfectly woven masterpiece provided a chilling, yet relaxing soundtrack. Along the 28th measure in the third movement, however, the trill notes that could almost always move me to tears were the only part of the bar I could hear. By measure 32, the entire song began to fade. Only a drugged up safe cracker opening a combination lock could duplicate how I must have looked as I focused to hear the music while I turned up the volume. My breathing was matching my elevated heart rate, panic stricken that I could not hear the music more clearly than as if it were being played 2 floors down and under water.

I needed this. I needed to know that I was just sick. That it was just the fever. That I could just sleep and it would all be better tomorrow. That, when I woke up, the people would stop tearing each other apart outside, the 911 line would clear up, and help would be on it's way. The floor would serve as my temporary bed as I used the speaker as pillow, forcing my ear into the sub woofer, demanding my lullaby. My eyes shook as I listened to the ballad play itself over and over, concentrating on every note I could. Even though I could only hear the highest notes resonating at first, eventually the entire piece could be heard. I had won the battle, my only weapon concentration. I could rest.

This morning served no other purpose than to remind me that, yes, I had fallen asleep upon the speaker and, no, this wasn't a nightmare. I pulled my head from the small, dark red puddle that had collected in the sub woofer, famished. Checking for any damage from my all night speaker sleeping might have been the proper, sanitary thing to do, but my craving demanded to be satisfied.

My eyes saw nothing but the fridge as I lurched unevenly toward the kitchen. My hands knew more than I did, opening the crisper and yanking the days old raw steaks from their spot like a mob boss. I placed them by the stove, not wanting to cook, but understanding that it had to be done. The next few minutes are a blur of blood and blackouts: Plastic and wax paper being ripped to shreds as I made my way to the blood-dripping shanks of muscle; the sinewy snap of pure animal flesh being pulled apart by my hands and teeth; the chewy, viscous feeling of the meat, barely chewed, falling down my throat. The clearest memory I have of this is seeing the package in shreds next to the stove, which I never even bothered to turn on.

I remember thinking I should have felt horrible. That I should have felt disgusting. But I didn't. For what it's worth, I did feel a bit unnerved when the undigested remains took the back exit out of my system 10 minutes later without me having a clue. A discovery I made by slipping in it while looking for more meat to consume. The best I could find was a can of Spam that had been in the cupboard since I moved in. The canned meat did no justice compared to what I wanted, but I clawed at it anyway, seeing the thick red blood spill out of my fingers as I cut them on the can and not caring.

But all of that was put on hold when the high-pitched squeal of tires on my street were heard. The grim crash that ended across the street would now perplex me and many others on the ground, in a way that had us standing and staring in awe. An awe so deep I stood there for what felt like hours. Until I became frightened. Frightened by a sound that was strange, yet familiar.

A gunshot.

I stood in my living room, stiff with fear. I wanted to run to the peephole, but even walking to the bathroom takes way too long anymore, yet leaves me feeling like I just ran 30 miles. So I listened. I listened as the shots got closer and closer, floor by floor. It was a semi auto, I could tell that. More infrequent pops rather than long, automatic-like rounds. Once the shots got to my level, with martial law in effect, I began to fear the worst.

I moved at a turtles speed, my knees continually locking up on me with every step, forcing me to stop and bend it a few times before taking another step as I made my way to the door. I'll admit, though, that the very distinct sound of gun shot tearing into human flesh, splattering the remains against the hallway walls, followed by a loud "thump!" of a body hitting the floor didn't make me wanna move that much faster anyway.

My curiosity peaked, however, when the gunshots remained in front of my door for a sustained time. I picked up my pace when the shots stopped, the loud sounds being replaced by furious banging at the door. I began wondering if the soldiers would give me a minute to gather some belongings before whisking me off to safety. Or if those in the hall were even soldiers in this brand new, lawless country that was forming. Then, I heard my name.

"OPEN THE DOOR!!" he screamed. The voice was familiar but I couldn't place it. When I finally made it to the door, the peephole proved ineffective. I could only make out the red shadows of what looked like bodies on the floor. A face took up most of my peephole vision. It looked left, then right, then left again. I could see his neck muscles working frantically with each turn. His fist kept up the barrage on my door the whole time. I managed to get out a weak request for patience while I fumbled with the deadbolt.

The lock barely let out a click of the release when the door flew open, sending me flying back on my ass. As quickly as it had opened, it was slammed closed again, the lock going back into the position it had been for days. I looked up to see Phil with his back against the door, panting. His signature leather jacket was covered in blood, much like the rest of him, and I don't think it was his own. I was surprised, but I'm not sure my face showed it. Or maybe he was just to preoccupied to notice, as he walked over to my stereo, ripped it out of the wall and shoved it in front of the door. I eventually pulled myself up to the couch, exhausted, but Phils pace never stopped. The kitchen table, the chairs, the end tables, everything that was in his immediate area went in front of the door.

After a couple of minutes, he stopped, leaving only the couch I was sitting on and the TV as the only objects not blocking the exits. He leaned on his newly made fort, pulling a black bandana out of his jean pants pocket and wiping his face of sweat and blood. Lighting a cigarette, he sat with his back to an end table on it's side, head back and smoking in silence. The heat from the embers of his smoke made me wince in nervousness.

"MoonlightSonata,huh?"Heaskedbetweenbreaths."Interesting choice for what's been going on out there. You seen it?"

I wanted to tell him about all the things outside my window alone, but the only thing I could muster out was "yeah", in more of a grunt than a spoken word.

He inhaled the cigarette deep and relaxed some more, sweat dripping down his face.

"You shouldn't leave your stereo on so loud, man. People are a bit nutty right now. Even the ones who aren't trying to eat you."

I agreed with him. I wanted to tell him about the phone company screwing me over, about the teleprompters that had it out for me, about all these crazy things that erupted since the president's announcement, but I simply couldn't convey it. I could only stare at the end of his cigarette in horror, wondering how it could feel like a sun was in my living room, yet be so small.

I heard him say something, but I couldn't focus on his words. Not when this ticking time bomb of embers was going to catch the rug on fire and turn this building into a blazing coffin, just like the one across the street. I heard him speak some muffled words then some elevated yelling, but I never took my eyes off the glowing death. My persistence paid off when I watched him wave in front of my face with both arms like a Airport runway guy, possess a look of terror on his face, and drop the smoke on the floor, causing the end explode like tiny fireworks all over the ground.

And, for the first time in days, I yelled. I yelled so loud and so high pitched, I think it could be considered a screech. He snuffed out the pending firestorm and I stopped, shaking my head in dizziness and confusion. And in that moment, all I wanted was to hug him.

Phil and I had been friends since we were kids and all through high school. After graduation we went down separate paths. I went on to the state college and life as an office drone. Phil joined the Army and traveled the world, earning accolades and medals the way I earned hemorrhoids and a spare tire. So when I ran into him at the local gas station two years ago, it was a welcome surprise. We talked and exchanged numbers, hugging upon our exit, which was weird. We never were the "huggy" type of people in school, but I guess growing apart after all these years, people tend to change. Ever since then we tried to get together to have lunch at least once a month. And every time, after the plates are cleared and we're done arguing about who's going to pick up the lunch bill, we hug.

And now, here he was. Pointing a gun to my head.

My arms reaching for him, I shuffled slowly toward him, still thankful for him saving me from the skin melting demise that could have been.

"NO!!" he screamed, stopping me in my tracks.

I didn't understand why he wouldn't accept my gratitude. Even though this damn cold made me feel like my mouth was full of peanut butter, I shuffled towards him again, trying to explain that I was just thankful. I tried to tell him that I had just been sick the past couple of days and that he was my hero for getting here, during all this hell, and taking me to safety.

"No . . ." he said. "You're one of them."

This didn't make sense to me, and I told him so. I was just sick. I hadn't hit anyone like those assholes on the news. I hadn't killed anyone like so many had outside my window. Surely no more than he had killed in the service. I couldn't believe that he'd cast our years of friendship away because I couldn't get proper treatment. Phillip's gun didn't waver, but remained pointed at my forehead. His eyes stared at me in pain and confusion, yet also apologetic as well. He didn't want to do this, but wouldn't hesitate. For the first time I wondered why he came for me of all people.

He began speaking, but his words were lost on me. I couldn't get past the smell of baked chicken wafting past me. He looked sad, his mouth flapping and his eyes welling with tears as he pointed a gun in my face and spoke in a depressed determination.

Our situation was suddenly a secondary issue when a high pitched screech, clear as day, could be heard outside the door, followed by rampant and violent banging on the walls. Phil spun around in a blur, pointing the gun at his crumbling, quick-made wall. As he shook in terror, the smell of a fresh cooked Roast Beef dinner climbed in and scratched at my nostrils. I raised my arms toward Phil, sure that he would want to go with me to find this mystifying, intoxicating meal that Had to be close and have lunch one last time before society fell . . .

I can't remember much after that. I don't know where Phil went, but we had to have found the food, cause I don't smell it anymore. Wherever he went, though, he must have been in a hurry, because he left his gun here. Every time I see it, now, I have this weird feeling. Like I should use it on myself for some reason. But why would I? Maybe he left it for me to deal with my dazed and confused neighbors, who seem to just be . . . Standing in my apartment, staring at the inferno across the street. I don't remember inviting them in, but they should leave. What if they catch my cold?

I hope Phil is OK.

Now, if you don't mind, I'd like to watch the fire.

The Snowwoman's Echolia

Doug Martin

The snowwoman had rocked all afternoon in the lawnchair.

High on Tickle Top, she held a can of hot oysters while the wind autographed her blueberry eyes. The child who lived in her heart and arteries always had already left for the city. Polka music was in the distance.

With face blindness, she looked right through you as you spoke, echoliaizing your every word, an autistic woman starting to weep on just another normal day in another normal year, when everyone you both had ever loved had died.

Killing the House

Doug Martin

The rattlers had moved west to the dumproad
inscribed with the ditch diggers' shovels and sweat.

Behind two backhoes spitting smoke in the Indiana summer,
the dirt the workers flung while repairing the covered bridge

was a ghost mist heading toward the parked Chevy.
In tall fingergrass near the back tire, Amy Sanford,

the mayor's daughter, was unzipping the pants of a sailor boy
with her teeth. He was setting down a bong full of Acapulco
Gold

he'd been lighting with a mirror held up to the sun.
He was thinking how when he got back home,

he'd tell all his friends that Amy Sanford's breasts
were like bathtub faucet handles he could turn on at will.

Her daddy would have taken a shotgun to him
if he had heard what words were said.

We were picnicking with stale bread and hamburger
out behind the barn. Above us, a cropduster paraquated

the fields of marijuana. Your shirt was monogrammed

with the letter D like a half-moon sewed into its pocket.

It was not my initial. We bicycled up the dumproad
in the heatsnap of August, and I half-jokingly called
your breasts the raw hamburgers of God. You playfully chased
me.
We saw two snakes cross over then weed themselves in a ditch.

When we got to the driveway, our three-year-old son
was rocking in the swing in a flannel shirt, way too hot

for this time and season. In the guest-room, your mother
was still piano lessoning the nun whose son had just died

next door in the conflagration. Our three-year-old son,
with spaghetti dangling from his mouth, believed

that the one bedtime story of that house across the lawn
would therefore always be death. We agreed.
We agreed and then he pointed at your father's house

with its b.b. gun-splattered windows and peeled aluminum
siding.
"Did the snakes kill this?" he asked.

"The neighborhood boys," you said.
I thought of the workers down at the bridge,

and how the sailor boy, like any other half-drunk, teenage kid
with money, could get nervous, jealous as hell until something
went wrong.

Flooring his car at 60 miles per hour, through all the
construction signs,
he could have plummeted fifty feet to the water.

It would have been like the time you left me for another man in
another city.

But no. That was like no other time.

Goodwill

Catie Spicer

Squares and bad seventies couches.
  Ribbons tie it all together.

Red coats,
  Nine irons,
  Brown Bowling Balls.

Happy,
  Just like the Movies.

Dumb, Little Sister

Megan K. Freeman

I couldn't cry at the wake. No matter how much I willed it, I just couldn't cry. So I resigned myself to embracing friends, acquaintances, and strangers, tenderly patting their hair and rubbing their shuddering backs. They felt like feeble babies in my arms and my exasperation made me disgusted with myself. So I took a deep breath and focused, once again, on the line of sullen-looking people I would still have to greet and console. I felt empty, but the thought that my sister's stiff body lay only a foot away in a shiny coffin sent chills down my spine periodically.

Later that afternoon, I let my body fall heavily on top of my bed and closed my eyes. I couldn't remember whom I had spoken to that day, or even what I had said to them. All I knew was the aching throb in the balls of my feet from having stood in heels for several hours and the sudden relief of taking them off. I longed for a massage but my head was too clouded. I rolled onto my back, allowing the silence to envelope me and I was soon asleep.

Disoriented, my blurry eyes searched for the dim red glow of the digital alarm clock. It was 9:45 P.M.; I had been asleep for three hours. Or, was it four? I rubbed my eyes, brushing the crust and makeup residue from the corners. The television was usually on in my father's study, while Mom would gab on the phone with Mrs. Pennington across the street about new deals on hydrangea bulbs at the garden nursery, new book suggestions for the neighborhood club, and of course, each and every one of their children. Allison would be listening to music so loud that it would blare through her headphones. But, I heard nothing at all except for my own steady breathing.

Venturing out of my room, I found that I was completely alone. My parents were gone and had left no note, no trace of having been there recently at all. I knew I ought to have phoned them, but the eeriness of the empty house had become serene. I maneuvered slowly to the kitchen and slid onto one of the stools, placing my elbows on the countertop.

There she was, Allison in her nine-year-old form, seated beside me, only six. My elbows barely reached the top of the counter the way Allison's did so comfortably. Mom had placed steaming plastic bowls of Mac & Cheese in front of us both and I noticed that Allison had received a metal fork, where as I was given a large plastic one with my own teeth marks in it. I grasped Allison's forearm in protest.

"Mama! I want a big girl fork too," I screeched.

"Ew Olivia, your fingers are sticky," lamented Allison, shaking her arm free of my grasp.

"Girls, cut it out and eat your dinner or no dessert," sighed Mom. I pouted until I schemed to exchange our silverware when Allison wasn't looking. I was always so confident that I could outsmart her.

"Mom, Olivia took my fork!"

"Did not!" I felt a hard pinch on my leg and a tumult of tears and bickering quickly followed. We were both sent to our bedroom, stomachs growling.

I opened my eyes, the bowls of steaming macaroni, Allison's thin arm in my sticky grasp, and my all-consuming jealousy of her dissipating like dust particles. I examined my hands: the chipping pink polish on severely bitten nails, the scar from thumb surgery after a dislocation in the volleyball game against South, the fading freckle in the middle of my left palm. Disenchanted with the damage of twenty years, I pushed off the stool and wandered into the adjoining living room.

Nothing was out of place. Various issues of Ladies' Home Journal and Time Magazine were strewn artfully upon the spotless glass surface of the coffee table. Owl blankets were draped in perfect folds over the backs of the black leather sofas. I felt my chest tighten as I carefully sat down on one of the cushions, aware that my weight could disrupt the order. I sat up straight, my hands placed symmetrically on each knee. I had forgotten that I was still wearing panty hose. I began to trace my fingers lightly down to my ankles. I remembered the first time I tried on panty hose after I was of the age to dress myself. My usual choices were considered by most on the "boyish" side.

"Why do you wear those?" I asked, a pertinent and curious twelve-year-old. I was leaning dangerously far over the couch's armrest as I watched Allison, radiant with the excitement of her first high school dance, descending the staircase.

"They make your legs look smooth, dummy," she laughed, sending her plethora of soft blonde curls bouncing about her.

"Weird. Can I try them on?"

And so we spent the short time before her date arrived, trying to put a pair of panty hose on me without tearing a hole or falling over. Allison showed me how to roll them all they way down to the foot part first, then to step in, and finally, to carefully roll them up each leg without snagging them on your nails or a bracelet. When we finally succeeded after several minutes, I pranced around for her amusement until she was red in the face with laughter. I felt an acute sadness at the sounding of the doorbell, which summoned her to her big night and to her date. I struggled to stay awake for her return, but when she did come home, I was utterly captivated when she regaled me with how she won her brilliant satin Junior Prom Queen sash, how she danced with her date Robby in front of the whole school, and most of all, how she smiled so broadly, revealing her gleaming white teeth. I leaned so far over my bed, enchanted by her story, that I fell off and bruised my knee. She promptly went downstairs and brought me up an ice pack and a plate of Oreos with a cup of milk; my absolute favorite.

I stared straight ahead, my eyes blankly on the staircase. Silent tears cascaded down my cheeks. I didn't move for several minutes until I registered a tingling in my fingertips. I had been rubbing them against the panty hose so hard that they were raw.

Shutting the door to the upstairs bathroom was unnecessary, but I did it anyway. I turned the cold faucet to a medium pressure and let my fingers graze the streaming column of water, as if it was made up of harp strings. Grasping the edge of the basin, the water still running, I let my head fall back slowly. A guttural, choking noise escaped from my throat and again the tears flowed, dripping one by one off my upraised chin and onto the front of my black chiffon dress. I remained like this, though now swaying slightly back and forth, until my neck began to ache. I avoided my gaze in the mirror and instead turned the faucet off. Sniffling quickly, I then felt for the zipper of my dress between my shoulder blades and let it fall at my feet. It looked like a giant ink stain through my blurred vision.

Wearing only panty hose, I found my way back to the edge of my bed in the darkness, shuffling my feet until I felt my knees prod into the mattress. I took out my ponytail holder and let it drop somewhere beside me. Too weak to get under the covers, I let the cold air from the open window singe my naked skin as I lay on my side, observing the emptiness of Allison's untouched bed only a foot away. I knew exactly how her sheets clung to her body, how she liked to sleep on her stomach, the way her leg would dangle slightly over the edge no matter how cold the room was.

She was on her back, arms extended like Christ on the crucifix, her chest rising and falling deeply.

"So, what was it like?" I asked timidly, praying the darkness of the room hid the blush forming on my cheeks.

"It was . . . well it was amazing. But it hurt too. I don't know, Olivia, it was just, wow." I propped myself up with an elbow, cupping my chin in my hand. I suddenly grew very conscious of my oversized flannel nightgown and long socks. I felt very young.

"Was it awkward, you know, after you did it?"

"No of course not. Bobby told me he loved me and I told him I did too. Then he held me until we realized that it was past midnight." She suddenly looked alarmed. "You didn't say anything to Mom or Dad, right?"

"No."

"I mean it Olivia, if they found out they would flip a shit."

"I said no, Jesus."

"Okay, okay. Well someday you'll know what it's like. Just make sure you do it with someone you love and who loves you, like Bobby and me. Olivia?"

I laid in silence, her words resonating as I imagined making love on a beach with a tanned surfer, then in a candlelit bungalow with a romantic Frenchman with hair past his shoulders, and even under the school bleachers with Bobby himself. He was the star pitcher of the baseball team and I felt enthralled and guilty for thinking about Allison's boyfriend that way. My particular arousal with the latter fantasy made me panic and so I made my eyes into slits and peered over at Allison to see if she was still awake. She was not. Relieved, yet distraught, I chastised myself silently for getting carried away until I too fell asleep.

I rolled onto my back. I was seventeen and still a virgin. And I was now without the one person I could count on as my confidante. When at last it was my turn to stay out past midnight, I would have to come home, careful not to stir my parents, dizzy with love and sore with lust only to mull over it all alone. My chest began to heave, rising and falling in violent chokes and I quickly grabbed a pillow, shoving my face into it and screamed. I screamed for all that I had lost, all that I was losing and didn't even realize. I screamed for her leg pinches, her bouncing golden curls, her sisterly advice that I pretended not to take. And suddenly I stopped. The quiet encased me, petrified me; it was as if my voice had been drowned in the wrenching undertow of an ocean, rendering me silent for weeks.

In the final days of her life, Alison had stopped talking as well. It started sometime after Bobby had broken up with her right before graduation for an undetermined reason, which she soon found really to be a pert, big-chested blonde on the dance team. In a fit of tears, she related to me the nature of their final conversation. Bobby had never really loved her and he had just wanted to see what she was like in bed. When Allison retorted, he simply said it was over and that she was a little too chunky for his taste.

That summer was hard on Allison. We all tried to comfort her in various ways. I would buy her magazines and her favorite colors in nail polishes using money from my paycheck as a café barista for the local bookstore. She would sift through them obediently under my gaze, though she was clearly feigning interest for my sake. Mom would sometimes give her breakfast in bed on neatly laid out trays with fragrant sprigs of baby's breath or lilac from her garden in a miniature vase. At first, Allison would thank her and take great efforts to get rid of the food as if she had eaten it.

I watched her once from the outside our room as the door was slightly ajar. She took several bites from the toast and without chewing it she would extend her tongue and deposit the small pieces in a napkin. I watched her rise up and disappear, only to return to her bed at the sound of the toilet flushing. After awhile, Allison brought this ritual to family dinners, concluding each meal with fistfuls of partially chewed steak, potatoes, anything, in leaky napkins. She would sneakily spit the food out whenever the attention was on someone else. Mom and Dad were oblivious as usual but, I marveled that she thought she was getting away with this unnoticed by me.

One day after work, I sat at the kitchen counter, propping myself up with my elbows. I was particularly exhausted that day, but my mother, preoccupied lately with Allison did not notice. It had taken a physical change in Allison for her to notice that something was wrong. Allison's once glowing skin was now taut over her jutting collarbones. Her nail beds were perpetually blue. Her pallor was yellowish and her dulled eyes were rimmed with purple. She was a sort of negative of her former self. She lurked around the house silently, if she left her room at all. By July she had stopped pretending to be a real person. She barely went through the motions.

"Hi O, how was work?"

"It was really shitty actually. My boss has been such a prick lately," I responded dejectedly, hopeful for some sympathy. There was a pause. I looked up and saw that she was perched over the kitchen sink, looking absentmindedly out of the small window outlined with fluffy yellow curtains. I could see her thoughts tracing elsewhere in her reflection the window made against the opaque darkness of that night.

"Mom!"

"Huh? Oh sorry, what was that about your boss?"

"Don't worry about it."

"I'm sorry O, I'm just really worried about Allie. We're already in mid-July and she hasn't gone out to see any friends, let alone find a job. I know she had a rough time with the Robby stuff, but I don't understand why she's still so upset. I'm also not sure if she's eating.

She's gotten so thin," she said, wringing a dishtowel out over the sink until it was more than devoid of moisture. "It's just not very normal."

I felt a surge of anger rising to my cheeks. I couldn't believe how ignorant my parents were, especially her. I also resented the fact that I had become a sort of shadow of a person in their eyes when it was Allison who wanted just that. I left the kitchen and went to sit out on the porch swing, letting the door clatter loudly behind me. My mother did not follow me out.

I swung myself lightly on the swing, pushing with my bare toes. The warmth of the arm and the steady rhythm of the rocking calmed me. Unwillingly, my thoughts shifted to Allison. I had woken early that day before I had to get ready for work. I observed her, feebly tucked in her sheets. Her leg didn't stick out anymore because she slept with her body compacted in a ball. The sight of her made me cringe, where it used to cause a fervid mixture of admiration and jealousy

Pushing with my toes more vigorously, the swing's bolts began to creak with the force. What the hell was so special about Bobby to make her do this to herself, to our family, to me? I bolted upright, hell bent on finding out.

In a whir, I was upstairs and standing above her curled body.

"Allison. Allison!" Her eyes opened, but she did not look up at me. She blinked slowly. "We need to talk right now."

"I am sleeping Olivia." She sounded so precise. She never used to talk that way.

"No, now Allison," I said, grasping her thin forearm. She pulled away, but my grip was much stronger. "What the fuck are you doing?"

She sat up slowly. Her pajamas hung loosely off her bony shoulder. She said nothing. This enraged me more.

"Do you know what you look like? Do you think I don't see the weird shit you do at dinner? What is the matter with you? Bobby is not that-"

"Don't." I had not heard her speak with such energy in a long time. I could see I was getting a rise from her and this invigorated me. She began to stand.

"No, don't you walk away from me," I said, blocking her waifish body from moving further. I saw her eyes welling. My voice softened. "I think you need some serious help, Allie."

"Don't be ridiculous, Olivia. You have no idea."

"No idea of what?" I said, encouraging her.

"No idea what it feels like to have your heart broken. Now leave me alone," she retorted, receding back into her covers.

"Wow, that's fair. Honestly, I don't give a fuck what I do or do not know according to you because you are clearly sick. How do you not see that?" She nestled her head against her pillow and spoke no more. I stared at her for several minutes until at last I stripped off my work clothes, throwing them in the corner, and got into my own bed seething.

The next morning began the same way as the one before. Except even though I had woken early, I did not stay to watch my sister. I showered and dressed as quickly as possible. I caught a glimpse of her as I stormed out; she hadn't changed positions from the night before. Fuck you Allie, I thought to myself as I slammed the door.

I was in the middle of pouring a skim chai tea latté for one of my regular customers when my boss paged me over the store intercom.

"Jesus Christ," I groaned under my breath. I was certain I was about to be reprimanded for something futile, like forgetting to refill the lids or packets of honey. It was always something like that. I untied my apron and chucked it on the back counter. I punched the code to the employee lounge and took a deep breath in preparation to meet my boss without erupting.

"Olivia," he said awkwardly. "I'm afraid there's been an accident."

Some time had passed; I had no idea how much. I sat in the sterile hospital waiting room, staring at a battered issue of Highlights that had pen all over it. I observed the curvature of the letters. I traced them with my eyes. My parents were somewhere close by. I could here my mother's whimpers buried in my father's chest. The doctor and nurses cooing apologies, it all fell dead on my ears. I don't remember anything that day except for the Highlights.

When I was finally ready to hear and understand, I learned what had happened. Allison had been suffering from depression. This had manifested itself in anorexia and possibly bulimia, which had caused a condition called hypokalemia, in which her potassium levels were dangerously low. Combined with a slow heart rate and the several pills of hydrocodone, she went into cardiac arrest that night of our fight.

I was now seventeen, my life totally inert. My parents turned all their attentions to me but like everything else I blocked them out. They sent me to therapy sessions, put me on Prozac. I spoke to no one at school and one by one my friends dropped out of sight. Allison consumed me. There was not room for anything or anybody else. I guess that my silence for those following months was my atonement for having been her dumb, little sister. Her death affirmed only one truth; I had nothing to teach and all to learn.

Summer Job

Ashley Coffman

It was the summer of 2007, and I was coming dangerously close to finishing my degree in English at Wellsburry College, at which time I would have to find a job and probably a place of my own. All I had left was one semester of student teaching, and then I would graduate in December. At the time I was living with my Aunt Margaret who, despite her anal retentive cleaning habits and insatiable need to control every situation, spoiled me endlessly. It was the ideal living arrangement for any college student. But it wasn't going to last forever. Sooner or later I was going to have to start supporting myself. Unfortunately, this required money, something I didn't have.

I had been working various part-time jobs throughout summer and during the school year. But when classes came to a close at the end of the spring semester that year, I was sadly without regular employment. I had been writing for the Chronicle, the school paper, since February, and my editor asked if I wanted to stay on as a writer. I agreed to it because I liked working for the paper and I needed the money. Regrettably though, writers were tough to keep around. Students would apply and be hired, but as soon as stories were assigned they would drop off the face of the Earth like flies on a bug zapper. Because of the lack of dependable staff, Jeff, the faculty advisor, decided it would be easier to print just three issues during the summer instead of the usual ten. The pay just wasn't enough to get by. I would have to look for a second job.

One day I was trekking through the student union, on my way to the office, when I spotted a flyer advertising "the perfect summer job." It was three hours a day in the evening, four days a week, and paid six bucks an hour plus benefits. And all I had to do was sit at a desk and call alumni. I applied in the Career Center and had an interview two days later. The following Monday was my first day on the job. It seemed pretty agreeable at first. Everyone I worked with was a student and my age. We worked in the phone room, a clean, air-conditioned office across from the Arena. Each person had their own desk and computer and a nifty head-set. They sometimes played games to pass the time and brought in snacks. And because we didn't start until six o'clock, I got to sleep-in until noon everyday. I spent most of the first day going through training.

It didn't take long for me to realize that what I would actually be doing was technically considered telemarketing, a job I had never heard spoken of fondly. I would be calling the esteemed alumni specifically to ask for donations. But this was different, I convinced myself. This was for a university. It was a good cause, I thought. I loved school; I'm a geek. And I believed in the value of a college education. This wasn't a greedy corporation trying to bully people into signing up for credit cards or subscriptions to magazines they don't want. This was collecting funds to improve the quality of our school and help students like me earn their degrees. This was something I could get behind.

"Don't expect people to be nice to you," they told me. Oh boy. "But always be polite to them." This wasn't a challenge for me; my middle name is Polite. "And don't get discouraged. You're going to get a lot of no's before you get a yes." That's okay. I can handle rejection. I'm a trooper. I'm the first one to volunteer for the dirty jobs and the last one to complain. I can do this. I went through a few calling scenarios with Janice, the supervisor. I was thrilled to use the skills I learned while studying for my theater minor. It was just like acting. I had an objective and obstacle, even a script. Piece of cake, I thought.

"Ready to try calling?" said Janice.

I struggled nervously through the first few calls, my hands shaking the entire time. But eventually I got the hang of it. It was all done on computer with an automated system. There were several different pools of Alumni; we called them "prospects." We spent that first week asking people to renew memberships to the Alumni Association and kept track of our progress on a dry-erase board in the office. It was $30 for single memberships, $40 for couples, and $20 for young alumni, people who had graduated within the last ten years. We also called alumni who had donated money in the past and asked them to donate again. This wasn't too hard since most of them had made it a habit to contribute. When they refused, it was either because they couldn't afford it or they were unhappy with the administration. Quite honestly, I couldn't argue with them on either count. We called parents of students to ask them to donate to the Parents' Fund, which buys books for the library. Occasionally, someone would pledge, but the standard answer was that they were already paying enough in tuition. We also did courtesy calls to thank people for previous donations; this was my favorite because we didn't have to ask for money and people seemed to get a real kick out of it. I only ever got to do one of these, and I had to leave a message on an answering machine.

The standard procedure for asking for donations was to start with an introduction. This always involved asking the prospect to confirm their mailing address and employment information, whether we knew it was correct or not. Then we had to build a rapport by asking three open-ended questions, something like "How did you enjoy your time at the university?" or "When was the last time you were on campus?" or "Why did you choose Wellsburry?" After that, we would transition by telling the prospect about all the amazing new things that were taking place on campus and how they wouldn't be possible without the help of alumni. Then we'd stress how important the participation of alumni is the university. Then came the ask.

We were required to make three asks. In the first one, we would slyly suggest they "participate" in the university by giving a gift of X amount. We would already have three different amounts in mind. When they refused the first one, we'd attempt a second ask: suggest that they might feel more comfortable with Y amount, something lower. This was called top-down selling. If they rejected that, we would make one last bid: tell them that what we were really looking for was participation more than anything, and even Z amount would make a big difference. This was usually somewhere around $20 or $25. We always had to use words like "participation" and "gifts." We were never allowed to say "money." Sometimes they would pledge. Sometimes they wouldn't. Sometimes they would hang up. If they did make a pledge, the next goal was to get them to use a credit card. This was a big deal because it ensured that the gift was received right away, and because we callers got an extra $2 for every credit card we pulled in. If the prospect wouldn't use plastic, the other option was to send them a donation card in the mail which they may or may not send back with a promised check.

This was the plan. For three hours each night, we'd dial hundreds of numbers, speak with dozens of unsuspecting people, and listen to countless answering machines. On a good night, a caller might get a handful of pledges. I could usually manage a couple. Until we started on the non-donors pool, that is. This was by far the toughest group. These were people who had never donated to the school before and probably never would. They didn't have much patience and really didn't like telemarketers. Most of the time, I didn't make it through all three asks. I usually got shot down after two. But I was always nice and apologetic, no matter how rude they were to me. Generally this didn't amount to much more than a cold response or a hang-up. But eventually it happens; you come across that one person who brings you nearly to tears. Everyone tells you not to worry about it. Shrug it off.

"It's not like you're going to ever meet this person face-to-face."

I got my call about two weeks into the job, from the non-donor pool. I had been dialing for a couple hours and having absolutely no luck. But, like a trooper, I maintained my happy face. "Smile and dial," they say. At some point, I called a man who had graduated in the 70s, which meant he had to be at least in his 50s. I did my introduction and ran through my spiel like normal and finally made it to the first asked.

"I was wondering if you'd like to participate tonight, sir, with a gift of, say, $50," I asked. I was low-balling it. The response was immediate.

"Let me tell you something," he said. Uh-oh. My throat began to tighten, but I decided to listen patiently, let him get it off his chest. His voice was quiet and deliberate. "My wife has Alzheimer's. She's fifty, and she's had it for three years. She is not doing well at all. Yesterday I found out through a letter in the mail that my taxes are going to double to $5,000. Five-thousand. I had to leave my job for one that pays half as much so I could stay close to my wife. Our kids live far away, and there is no one here to take care of her except me . . . Now, does it sound to you like I have money to give away?"

The Alzheimer's was what struck me. I thought of my maternal grandmother. She had been diagnosed two years earlier with a rare form of it called Pix disease. She had tiny strokes that cut off the oxygen to certain sections of her brain. This was slowly causing it to die. The night before, my mom called to let me know they were taking my grandmother off her meds because she had begun to soil herself. She couldn't feed or dress herself anymore. She sometimes didn't remember family or friends. She didn't have any short-term memory left at all. Her personality had been severely altered too. Once a graceful and ambitious lady, she was now a helpless child.

"No, sir. It doesn't sound like you have any money to spare," I said.

"That's right. I don't."

"I'm so sorry," I said. "I understand . . . about your wife, I mean . . . My grandmother has Alzheimer's too."

"Then you know how bad it is," he said.

"Yes, sir, I do," I answered.

My Uncle David had decided to move both my grandparents in with him because neither one was capable of caring for themselves or each other. I thought of my grandfather. His heart was broken. He had to watch the love of his life die a bit more every day. My uncle would sometimes find him standing in the kitchen by himself, weeping. And there was nothing that could be done to stop any of it. There was no hope. No magic cure . . . just the inevitable.

"And I—I'm sorry about your taxes," I stammered.

"Five-thousand!" he exclaimed. "Found out in the mail, yesterday."

"I-I really am. I'm so sorry," I said again. I meant it. "And about your job too. I can only imagine how rough that must be."

"Then you understand why I can't give you any money," he replied.

"I do. I understand completely," I said. "And . . . if there's ever anything Wellsburry can do for you . . ." I didn't really know what the college might do to help, but it seemed like the right thing to say.

"Oh . . . no," he said. He began to soften a bit. "I get by alright on my own."

"Okay . . ." I said. "Well, I'm really sorry we bothered you. And . . . I . . . I really hope things get better for you and your wife."

"Well . . .," he said. "Thank you."

"Okay . . . You have a good evening, sir." I said. And I hung up.

I sat for a moment with my head in my hands. I could feel that my face was hot and tears were starting to well in the corners of my eyes. I choked it back for a second, breathed in, trying to get a grasp on the moment. I finally managed to push the conversation out of my head. I'll cry later, I promised myself. After a couple minutes, I had composed myself enough to make the next call. There was still half an hour left on my shift. It's not what I wanted to do. I wanted to quit. I wanted to walk out right then. But of course that wasn't an option. So like a good trooper, I finished the shift. I didn't make any pledges that night. I guess that didn't really matter much, though. I didn't care. As I was getting ready to head home, Janice stopped me.

"You okay?" she asked, and I spilled the whole story. "Aw, don't worry," she said patting me on the shoulder. "You'll never meet these people."

Doesn't matter, I thought as I walked out the door. We already know each other.

White Space

Kilah Maree Galvan

The clock ticks slowly
incessant
repetitive
the teacher rambles on about something
I will forget after a test
I feel like I've been submersed into the latest episode
of "Peanuts"
I don't think it's even words
    my teacher is speaking

Cleared away
nothing but a pristine sheet of paper
and a pencil remain
    on my classmates' desks

I look up
what have I daydreamed myself through?
the teacher is writing on the chalkboard
I hoist my stuff under my desk
 copying my classmates

I look up
yellow chalk branding my eyes
screaming at me from the black board
which is really green

"What do you want to be when you grow up?"

Oh, shit!
anything but this
please, I will write twenty pages about anything in the world
just don't ask me this
I peer around me
all ready pencils are scribbling faster than my mind can even think
my classmates are writing down their futures
they must dream better than me
        bigger and faster
so sure of what they want

what do I want to be?
how am I supposed to know this?
let me think now
I know what I don't want to be

I don't want to be a stripper
        a drug addict, an alcoholic
I don't want to be someone who is feared
like anyone would ever fear me
I don't want to be a bum
        a menace, a taker

"When I grow up," I write
when the teachers eyes land on me
taunting me with my unknown, unsure future

I want to be a member of the Peace Corps
I want to be a doctor
        a lawyer
I want to be a movie star
        a child advocate
Maybe I will be a historian
study the pyramids in Egypt
trek through the concentration camps in Europe
journey on the Great Wall

Lowell R. Torres

I want to be a writer
I want to be a therapist
a rebel with a cause
a crusader to save the world
a helper
a giver
a lover
a fighter
a protector

I want to be a mother
a wife
Well, do I want to be a wife…?
I think of all the women I know
who carry wife as a label
This is the future; I'll figure it out then

Tap, tap, tap
the teacher's finger is on my paper, ordering me to write
"I want to be," I force myself

Sure, I can change my mind tomorrow
but I don't want to lie today
I want to write the truth
I shake my head, my mind all ready trying to wander away
my attention span shrinking with each second that I grow older

Maybe I want to be a teacher?
No, I don't think so
Maybe a chef?
Nah, you have to be able to cook
and macaroni and cheese with hot dogs
doesn't count

"Time," my teacher calls
my classmates put their pencils down
every single one of them look smug

like they are in on some secret
and I will never be able to guess it
they're all so put together
they know exactly what they want

I look down at my paper
I can't turn it in like this
What do I want to be when I grow up?

papers start passing forward
I use the vast white space in front of me
    my future as blank as my paper
and scribble, without thinking
"I just want to be me."

New Direction

Dusty Anderson

Their stomachs were queasy. Were they about to get fired? Really? Till this second, it was harmless fun and filmmaking with friends. Something altered the genetic-normalcy of their professional careers for this moment to exist.

"I don't feel like you're that into it," a slight Indian accent revealed to a dumb-founded, 21 year-old Production Assistant/ Editor through a cheap cellphone. This job looked like a ticket to the big time; granted, it was a small film, but it would be a Bollywood release, which means people would see it, and credits would be noticed, probably. That's assuming the film is good. Adam signed-on to the project for experience, even though life was very hectic. It was much easier to say "Yes" when Braden was adamantly involved.

Adam's stomach rumbled again, contemplating a revolt, when his eyes darted to Braden. Adam had found a nice place among the rack of DVDs to rest his eyes while the bad vibes infiltrated the phone; how many Scorsese films are there? Braden's room was relaxing and fun most of the time: it would have been paradise for a 14-year-old because of all the movie posters, videogames, unopened toys, and endless rows of DVDs and Blue-Rays. But right now it was unsettling. From the first ring, Braden had been aware of who was calling, and since Adam feebly uttered "Hello?" he could feel his best friend's piercing eyes. He finally looked and met them. Bright blue and unforgiving a lot of the time, yet cautious now, they forced Adam to admit the severity of the situation in a non-verbal sort of way. Braden and Adam had a way of not being able to hide anything from each other. Only because they couldn't.

"Well, I guess . . . Yeah . . . Bye." Adam sighed tremendously.

"What the fuck, man?"

"He just took us off the schedule. We haven't been getting the updates or emails . . ." "'Just took us off the schedule.'" Braden barely believed it. "Both of us?"

"And, he uh, forced me to call him, but he's 'so busy,' he had to call me back, uh, so he can say," his voice was shaking a bit despite his resistance, "he doesn't want us to be a part of it anymore."

"Took us off the schedule." Braden's following pause gave him superior energy for "Son of a Bitch!" He stood still for a moment.

"He said he'd put me back on if I, uh, 'got the fire . . . the passion, in me again.' But I never lost it. What does he mean? I can't speak for you, but I think it was time to part ways, even before all this," Adam appeared reluctant to say. A spell of silence held the room against its will. He found some courage and mocked Jayin's slight accent: "'You're just not that into it.' What the hell? I mean, I've been 'into it' for 3 months now, staying over in his cramped den going blind from that giant screen learning that damn editing program . . ."

"'No, you're definitely not into it,'" Braden picked up the mock-accent now. He'd actually gotten pretty good at it. "'I probably should have fired you much earlier for your hard work.'" This got Adam smiling. "'What a dipshit I am for keeping dedicated people" and that got a chortle. Adam's shaking was relieved and his hard-to-remove smile finally appeared.

Jayin's den was homey enough, though cramped, with the kitchen just a few steps away and a large, flat-screen TV hanging on the wall in the adjoining room directly behind him. Even though the sound was muffled, Adam managed to follow the storylines of the ridiculously feigned MTV reality shows that Kulik and Anya, Jayin's son and daughter, always watched too loud. It reminded him of his attempts at homework at his parent's house until Jayin ordered his kids to "turn it down." Adam felt in the way. The family sacrificed a lot tiptoeing around him at 11:36 p.m. when all they wanted was a glass of water. Jayin insisted, as he was very accomplished in the art, so Adam frittered away quiz preparation and biology reading time to be further skilled in creating gun muzzle flashes and synching up fight sequences. His college career was suffering. But he was making movies; it had been totally worth it.

"If I knew he was going to can me all along, I could have an 'A' in Biology right now instead of a 'C—.' Jayin's got kids, right? Don't he know the difference between 'A' and

'C—?'"

"He probably teaches his kids to use throat-punches on their teachers if they give 'em bad grades." Braden adopted a cocky, stock-straight posture. "'Oh, hey Teach . . . What's that? I got a 'D+' in History?'" He mimics a quick upper-cut with a jabbing motion. "'What's it now? 'C'?

'C—?'" Another jab, this time directed toward an imaginary crotch. "That's right. I thought it said 'A.'" Braden and Adam were back to themselves now as Adam was adding.

"If that don't work, they could just say 'Don't you know who my Dad is? He's in movies! Really bad, Bollywood movies!'"

"'His name is Jayin,'" Braden kept up the mockery. "'Oh, you haven't heard of him? You don't know who he is? You say I still have a 'D+'? Oh, I'm causing a disturbance, am I?'" He relieved Adam's tension and they both were thankful. This was the normal atmosphere of a hang-out session at Braden's.

"'No, I'm sorry, Jayin junior, the reason you have a 'D+' is that your Dad is too busy getting sprayed with coconut oil for his training close-ups to ever help you with your History.'" Adam laughed a little at himself for that one. "'Besides, if he were around to help you, his oily hands couldn't pick up the History book.'" He mimicked what looked like a classic Jerry Lewis, clumsy-waiter routine.

"If he could get past his mirror," Braden faintly flexed his breasts, replicating Jayin, adding to the ridiculousness. Now Adam was laughing out loud and flexed his pathetic, pasty biceps. He even asked 'You know where the weight room is?' before nervousness regained ground and sent a shock to his bladder, and he skidded to the bathroom.

"Where you goin'?" Braden asked. They'd just gotten back to their old rhythm.

"Hold on" he blurted, while pushing open the bathroom door and finding the light. "I gotta pee!" Adam's bladder was always working more than it needed to; something that reminded him several times a day to visit the doctor. Now it was his brain informing his body that he needed to relax a moment. He'd gone back to his old, joking, quirky self without any reflection on the matter—he lost his job. At this realization, Adam caught his image in the mirror; his smile dissipated before he looked up. Only the cold eyes of his reflections told him "You're in serious trouble. This was your gateway." He sighed heavily as the thought clanged around his skull. His reflection, without a doubt, said "Way to fuck up" without saying anything. He was always silently hard on himself, even if it wasn't always vindicated. His stomach wrenched again. What would he say to people back home? He didn't want to think about it. He lifted the toilet ring and pissed.

The ease of the bladder relieved Adam's reversion of dismay, and then thoughts of the last film-shoot rose up. Jayin, covered in coconut oil, surrounded by a young girl with a camera aimed upon him, a young man bouncing the sunlight onto his chest with a crude, sunlight-bouncing device (which made his trying-way-too-hard muscles look like a swimming pool with pubic hair), a pair of college kids, one holding a fish-pole microphone out over him, and the other one meticulously keeping just enough slack on the microphone wire, not too much, which could get tangled up and not too little which, inevitably, resulted in the former bobbing the mic into the screen or occasionally the wire-wrangler himself, was in the center of all this and glowed in the spotlight.

Adam thought about how everyone at that exact moment was entirely focused: mainly upon Jayin but also incredibly concentrated on their jobs. Almost too hard. He laughed, continued to urinate. The thought of Jayin's swimming chest muscles and the poor camera operator who had to film it, in High Definition, no less. And everyone so alert to every detail, bouncing back and forth on the balls of their feet, all around this guy who absorbed every inch of it. Even Kulik, Jayin's son, was beneficial that day; at his home, he basically watched TV unsupervised until he found some form of annoyance he could indulge in. He held cue cards and helped keep abreast of the shot-sheet and script, when he could. It was surreal: inside the specter it was all dedication. From outside, it looked like a cartoon. Did everyone really expect this movie to be . . . yes, they did. Even Adam did, was hopeful, was counting on it. But during the shoot everyone seemed to forget the reason they started doing this: for fun! He and Braden were the only ones that cut loose from time to time, cracking jokes in-between takes, remembering the milieu of their own short-film productions. They could get the others to participate in the light-heartedness and good times, but only if they really worked at it. What was the point of following your dream, anyway, if you couldn't enjoy it?

A thought nailed the back of his eyes and pushed them to the mirror. He looked shocked. He knew why they were fired. After the zip-up and putting the seat down, Adam washed his hands, slowly, wringing every print, every cuticle, every finger, deliberating.

Braden warmed up the new Mario Party back in his room in hopes to keep the good vibes going. Adam always ran out of the room at inconvenient times to take a piss. Braden figured Adam's bladder was nonexistent, forcing urine straight to his penis, so he excused him. Plus, Adam was his friend. And better to leave the room and make awkward lapses then make messes on his couch.

Adam reentered the room striving to show no emotion. Eventually Braden busted him. It was a hopeless attempt. In an increasingly isolated society, people mutter and clamor their inner desires and emotions within the vicinity of their own head. But Adam and Braden were frontiersmen for expression and exploring the avenues of the new-found emotional man; they could actually solve personal, social problems in an objective and positive manner, and they learned a lot about themselves in the process. And each other.

Reaching for the Wii-mote, Adam sat on the small couch diagonal to Braden in a videogame chair; Braden witnessed a perplexing look on his friend. Something wasn't right. Did he pee on the floor? Was he afraid to say something about it? In an entirely joking manner at first, Braden asked "What's wrong?"

Adam sort of shrugged his shoulders, smirked a little, and made a half-grunt-half-mumble that basically said "Naw, nothing, it's . . . nevermind . . ."

"Seriously. You alright?"

Adam took a breath.

"Adam?"

He breathed out. Slowly. It was time for Braden to know. "You remember the last day we filmed with Jayin? Had the whole crew there?"

Braden bubbled out a laugh. "And we had to get 5 different angles of his oil covered chest," he couldn't help but laugh, "and he glimmered like that girl from Fast Times at Ridgemont High that got out of the swimming pool in slow-mo?" He lost it now. Adam did too. Probably because he pictured Jayin in a red bikini, slowly walking toward him, seductively. Now he was disturbed. Then he remembered why he spoke.

"You remember toward the end of the shoot, before we left for the day, what happened in the car?" Adam had a serious tone. Braden's face crinkled in uproarious laughter. He remembered too.

Finally catching his breath, Braden said "He forgot his son!" and laughed a bit more before taking up Jayin's accent again. "'Wasn't that a great shoot? I was breaking those blocks, then I was running up the hill, then I lifted those weights . . . '" he imitated a look of immediate horror upon his face, then said "'Where's my son!?'" Braden's face turned red and he leaned forward, he laughed so hard. Laughter was contagious, especially regarding Adam, if it came from Braden. He let out a few chuckles in spite of his remorse. Then Braden got most of the laughs out and started to calm down.

"Well, do you think that's why he fired us?" Adam seriously thought so.

"What!? Why?" Braden snickered once more but soon became responsive to Adam's tone. "We didn't lose his son. Did we?"

"No, we didn't, but what did we do when he thought he lost Kulik? Didn't we laugh?"

"Did you see his face!?" Braden started to laugh again. "How could we keep from laughing? That was hysterical!" Adam tried to throw the scolding-parent look on Braden.

"You laughed, too!" Braden said, defiantly.

"Yeah, and now neither of us have jobs. Seem like a coincidence?"

"Would he really hold that against us? His son was perfectly fine . . . he'd fire us for that?"

Though brief in existence for Jayin, and nonexistent for everyone else, his son had actually disappeared, and two of his employees laughed with glee at his vulnerable moment and terrified expression.

"He never actually lost his son," Braden said slowly and deliberately, as if taking a firm stance in his futile position. "Kulik was perfectly fine the entire time. You knew it, I knew it, Kulik even knew it, peacefully riding back to the house in a separate car." Braden's air understood how Jayin could be less than happy with he and Adam, but he rationalized the situation: "Jayin was so wrapped up in what 'he' did, and how 'he' looked, and how awesome 'he' was that 'he' forgot Kulik was ever there."

True. Jayin's parenting was below par. Jayin had a lot of investments and therefore a lot to take care of i.e. he had little time for the family. Adam thought it possible for Jayin to ignore Kulik, like the time he wanted help on a difficult math problem, but Jayin directed Kulik to Anya his older sister. Jayin was lining something out at the time, over the phone, (while Adam overheard the whole encounter while trying to edit) and it prevented him from helping. With a father who craves the limelight and bustles his children around in the movie-making-atmosphere, Kulik doesn't stand a chance.

"I'm not sure we had a right to laugh, Bray." Braden only stared hard at Adam's for his last remark. They didn't have a right to laugh. If Javin was someone they respected and cared for, laughing at him in his panicked moment of dread was not acceptable. They had laughed at Jayin when he thought he left his son behind at the film shoot. They laughed. It wasn't a laughing matter. Not for Jayin; it was serious. "I wouldn't want someone laughing at me if I thought I lost my kid. It's not right," Adam said. Braden thought this over.

"Well, don't feel bad because it could happen to you. Feel bad for the person just because it happened to them, because something bad happened to someone good that wasn't deserved" Braden reasoned. These words seemed to hit Adam because he indeed felt terrible for laughing, yet he wondered what allowed him to laugh at all. Did Jayin deserve his brief seconds of shock? Was it some epiphany that would awaken Jayin to his poor fathering? Maybe.

Maybe he'd be a better father for this. Adam and Braden wouldn't find out.

"Why did you laugh, anyway?"

"Hey, I wasn't alone! I saw you laughing" Braden retorted.

"I laughed because you laughed! I couldn't help it once I saw you laughing. And poor Jayin, he looked . . . so . . . horrified—"

"That's why I laughed!" Braden demonstrated what got him and Adam fired. Being the center of everyone's attention, having his needs carried out as if he had personal attendants, Jayin relished upon every compliment, felt more important with every order he gave, every call for "action" or when he told the camera operator to make sure "he" was the focus of the shot. That entire day had been about Jayin and his absorption of all that attention was making his walk more like a swagger, probably to accommodate for the tremendous weight gain above the neck. The crew noticed but it didn't distract them from their craft. Besides, Jayin wasn't purposely harming anyone, but he gloated for having everyone attend to him. Then his world tumbled to an intense reality, a scary notion that his own son, his legacy, had disappeared, that he'd forgotten him, that his son would know he'd forgotten him, and for a brief moment, he didn't know where he was or what was happening to him. And when the world reminded Jayin that he wasn't the only one functioning in it, Braden saw it as a dose of reality that was well prescribed. Jayin hadn't earned Adam or Braden's respect, so when karma crashed through, they could only laugh at the rebalancing of the universe, however inappropriate.

Works Cited

Fast Times at Ridgemont High. Dir. Amy Heckerling. Perf. Sean Penn, Jennifer Jason Leigh, Judge Reinhold, and Robert Romanus. Refugee Films, 1982. Film.

How Three Mice Became Three Blind Mice

Jessica Rossiter

One day, three mice brothers, Adam, Russ, and Sam, were sitting about in their den finishing breakfast.

When Adam Mouse stood up to get some oats from the shelf, he saw a tall spider coming into their den through the mouse hole.

"Eeeeek!!" Adam shrieked and dropped the bag of oats to the floor.

Sam and Russ followed Adam's eyes to the entrance hole and shrieked too.

"EEEEEEK!" They all said together.

The spider was so scared from their shrieks that he quickly turned and ran away.

"Did you see that spider?" said Russ. "It was so big! And it had ten legs!"

"Well, it was big, but everyone knows that spiders have only six legs," said Sam.

"No way! I counted them. It had twelve!" Adam argued.

"This is such a silly thing to fight about," Sam stated. "Especially, when I'm right. All spiders everywhere have exactly six legs."

"You're wrong! They have ten!" said Russ.

"No, you're wrong, because this one had twelve!" exclaimed Adam.

Soon, the mice were shouting loudly, "It had ten!"

"Six!"

"Twelve!"

Adam got so mad at his brothers that he picked up the bag of oats from the floor and threw it at them!

"Twelve legs, I say!"

Then Sam said, "Can you believe Adam threw that at us?

What shall we do to him?"

"We??" asked Russ, as he pushed Sam away.

This got Sam MAD, so he poked Russ right in the eyes!

Russ could not see then and shouted, "My eyes!"

He pushed forward with his fingers pointed straight at Adam's eyes, thinking it was Sam.

Soon Adam was shouting, "I can't see! How dare you!!"

He then moved forward with his fingers poised, pointing right at Sam's eyes.

They fell to the ground, and Sam called out, "Get off of me! I'm blind!"

What a sight it was for those who could see!

Three brother mice now were three blind mice.

They stumbled around angrily, blaming their blindness on one another.

Suddenly, the same spider appeared in the mouse hole and said, "An eye for an eye makes the whole world blind."

"By the way, we spiders have eight legs and eight eyes. Together, you three had six legs and six eyes. Because of your fighting, you have six legs, but no eyes."

The spider turned around and walked out of the mouse den, leaving the mice crying over what they had lost.

After a while, they could cry no more, and they had no more angry words for each other.

They decided that they would have to help each other to get up.

Soon the three blind mice discovered how much more they could do when they worked together. They began to speak out within their mice community about violence, and they even wrote a song.

Three Blind Mice.
Three Blind Mice.
See them work together
United now forever.
They all fought over a silly thing
And lost their sight while arguing
But learned the importance of being loving
Three Blind Mice.
Three Blind Mice.

Author Bios

Jared Yates Sexton received his MFA from Southern Illinois University and currently serves as an Assistant Professor of English at Ball State University. He is a former recipient of the Mary Reid MacBeth Short Fiction Award and has had his work appear in The Emerson Review, Relief, The Benefactor, Bull, among other journals.

Nathan Jones grew up in Rensselaer, Indiana. He is a retail pharmacist, finishing up an MFA in creative writing at Northwestern University. He has been published in *From the Edge of the Prairie* and *Borderlands: Texas Poetry Review*. "Rogues" is a story about some middle school kids, which takes place in that area.

Dalila Huerta graduated from Marian University-Indianapolis in 2009 with a B.A. in History, after attending Goshen High School in Indiana's Amish Country. Originally a Chicago native, she has grown to love and respect the sacrifice, struggle, and everyday beauty found in the Hoosier State—themes which she strives to highlight in all of her poetry.

Teal Schlueter has lived in Indiana nearly all his life. He bought a house in the Broad Ripple for the wonderful culture he enjoys from the Indianapolis neighborhood, as well as the closeness to downtown, Castleton, the highways, and the Monon Trail

Josh Green was born and raised and expelled from high school in Terre Haute. Recovered, he graduated college with honors and worked at newspapers around Indianapolis. He currently is a journalist and fiction writer living in Atlanta. His work has appeared in *The Adirondack Review, New South, Lake Effect, The Midway Journal, Bloodroot, Amarillo Bay, The Indianapolis Star* and recently placed second for the Kneale Award in Purdue University's 76th Annual Literary Competition. He covers the crime beat for a metro newspaper, adhering reluctantly to facts. This story was inspired by a gym in Broad Ripple.

J. Elaine Dyer was raised and educated in small Indiana towns before moving to the City of Broad Shoulders to earn an MFA in poetry from Columbia College Chicago, where she also teaches first year writing. Her work has appeared in various magazines and journals including *Phantom Limb*, *OVS*, and *Exact Change Only.* When she's not writing or teaching, she's watching Star Trek or reading poems.

Megan Hamand was born and raised in Indiana. She attended Indiana State University, where she studied English, creative writing and journalism. After college, she returned to her hometown in Northern Indiana, where she worked as a journalist at a South Bend advertising agency and publication company as the only writer for their two magazines. She currently works as a manager at KeyBank in Knox, Indiana. She's been published in *Terre Haute Living Magazine, Indiana English, Internationally Yours, Online Writing: The Best of the First Ten Years*, and was featured on Word Riot's Web site.

Russell Puntenney is an Indiana native, born and raised in Noblesville. He graduated from Indiana University in 2006 with a degree in Journalism and Philosophy and has been writing for most of his life. While in Bloomington he had poetry featured in the literary magazines *Fusion* and *Canvas* and also composed a weekly opinion column for the Indiana Daily Student called "RussellMania," and since then has covered the Indianapolis Colts for the now-defunct sports blog website Most Valuable Network and reviewed movies for the website of Indianapolis's NBC affiliate station, WTHR.

Lowell R. Torres was born in and raised throughout Northwest Indiana, from Gary to Valparaiso and everywhere in between. He studied history and creative writing at Indiana State University and Edge Hill University in Ormskirk, United Kingdom. He has been published in *The Glue Factory, The Grasslands Review,* and *Online Writing: The Best of the First Ten Years.* He lives in Bloomington with his wife and two children.

Tony Brewer has lived in Indiana all his life. His work has appeared in *Poetry Midwest, Bathtub Gin, Ichabod's Sketchbook, Beltway Poetry Quarterly*, the *Outsider Writers Collective*, and forthcoming in the anthology *And Know This Place: Poetry of Indiana*. He has also recorded several programs for The Poets Weave on WFIU Public Radio (www.indianapublicmedia.org/poetsweave/tag/tony-brewer). Tony is one-quarter of the all-Hoosier-poet performance troupe Reservoir Dogwoods (www.

IndianaPoetryTour.com). His first book is *The Great American Scapegoat* (2006) and his latest chapbook is *Little Glove in a Big Hand* (Plan B Press, 2010).

Thomas V. Nowak has been writing seriously for the last seven to eight years. He's taken summer writing courses at the Iowa Writers Workshop and at Butler University in Indianapolis. He is an active member of the Indiana Writers' Center and a continuing member of the fiction workshop. His stories have been published in *Oasis Journal 2006, Kaleidoscope, Colere,* and *Flying Island.*

Keoni Hooker has lived in Indiana since the age of 10. Originally from California, it took some time for Keoni to adjust to the culture shock of life in in the Hoosier State. It's steadily been upgraded from "weird" to "not too shabby." This is his first published work.

Catie Spicer is a resident of Fontanet, Indiana. She currently attends Indiana State University where she is majoring in English. Before returning to ISU this spring, she attended Vincennes University where she graduated with an Associate's Degree in English and a Certificate in Dance. While in Vincennes she was co-editor of the *Tecumseh Review* literary magazine and had the privilege of leading a seminar on how to foster a better writer's community on your campus at the Indiana Collegiate Press Association conference in 2007. Catie has had five poems previously published in *Northern Reflections* literary magazine, her high school's publication, and in the *Tecumseh Review*. She is very passionate about her writing as well as reading the work of her peers.

Doug Martin has had work appear in *Double Room, elimae, Hotel Amerika, Nimrod, Third Coast,* and other publications. A former Theodore Morrison Scholar at the Breadloaf Writers' Conference, and a past poetry editor of the *Mid-American Review,* Martin is the author of *A Survey of Walt Whitman's Mimetic Prosody* (Edwin Mellen, 2004).

Megan K. Freeman is a junior at Indiana University majoring in English with a creative writing concentration. In the 2009-2010 school year, her poem *A Trip to the Candy Whore* won poem of the week in the English department.

Ashley Coffman is is a Hoosier born and raised. She is a graduate of Indiana State University. She resides in Ellettsville, IN with her husband Kyle and works for Indiana University's Kelley School of Business. At the time of this publication, they are expecting their first child.

Kilah Maree Galvan has lived in southern Indiana since she was two years old. She graduated from IU and has since married and settled down in Bloomington where she is a stay at home mom to her beautiful little girl.

Dusty Anderson was born in Bowling Green and spent his time playing baseball and basketball very poorly. He moved to Patricksburg when he was eight years-old and eventually learned the art of the joke, which helped him cope with his parents divorce. He spent time in the woods as a kid and loved sitting next to a campfire. He's spent many Indiana nights putting wood on the fire, staring up at the stars, and drinking a few cold beers. He now loves spending time with his wife and daughter, when not preparing to be a teacher, and splitting wood when he gets the chance (when he's not writing).

Jessica Rossiter was born in Milwaukee, Wisconsin, but spent her entire youth in the town of Anderson, in Madison County. Upon graduating from high school, Jessica began a serious career as a "wanderer," traveling throughout the US, some of Europe, and later South America. Indiana is still her home when not traveling. Jessica has collaborated on stories with her five-year-old daughter to create such similar children's titles as: *Little Yellow Riding Hood, Three Little Pigs and a Not-So-Bad Wolf,* and *I Want to Be an Animal!*